TRIANSH
&
The Land of Immortals

MYST

INDIA • SINGAPORE • MALAYSIA

ISBN 979-8-89133-431-1

Contents

Chapter 1:

The Roadtrip

As the autumn season embraces Dehradun, the market area takes on a distinct charm. The air carried a hint of crispness. As the evening progressed, the market area was bathed in a gentle, warm glow from streetlights and the soft illumination of shops. A young girl watching from a distance noticed how an ice cream vendor skilfully constructed a cone with three flavours for a customer among the commotion. She silently begged her mother for a treat as she pulled at her mother's hand while staring at the alluring 3-tier ice cream. Her mother was busy bargaining with a shopkeeper over a frock; her drive to get a good deal was clear, but the small girl's efforts went undetected. Gradually, the girl's attention switched, now focused on a person standing behind the ice cream cart on the other side of the street, who too had their eyes glued to the delectable treat. Her attention was fixated on the mysterious figure, whose face was hidden by a hoodie and a mask, showing only a set of brilliant blue eyes. Standing at a commanding height of about 6'10" this person was dressed in jeans, a t-shirt, and a jacket. The girl was perplexed, wondering herself, "Why would a grown man be so fixated on an ice cream? He could easily cover the cost on his own." She noticed that he appeared to be aware of her observation, which caused him to lower his head, adjust his hood, and withdraw into the darkness of an adjacent alley with his hands safely tucked within. The young girl's focus returned to the alluring ice cream, and she continued to gently nudge her mother after he was no longer in view.

Five months had passed, and with that, the landscape had changed into a serene painting of a March night. The city of Dehradun was dozing out beneath a sparkling canopy of stars, but it was actually waking with the promise of adventure. Three close friends couldn't contain their excitement for the impending adventure, despite the peaceful surroundings. Their final exams for the 12th grade were completed the day before, something they had excitedly waited for. With careful preparation for this very occasion, their anticipation had been building for a while. They collaborated to make sure their preparations for the upcoming expedition were thorough and precise through the use of a conference call.

Arjun's voice rang out through the phone, full of astonishment and joy. "Guys... I'm still trying to wrap my head around the fact that this long-awaited day has finally arrived."

Arjun, a young kid with a slim build, stood around 5'7" tall and exuded a youthful vitality that was contagious.

"I absolutely know what you mean," Aditya said, joining in the excitement. "We've been planning this excursion since ninth grade, and it's fantastic that our parents have finally given the go ahead." Aditya, in contrast to his friends, had a stronger frame, standing 5'10".

Arjun couldn't help but describe his relatively simple process, saying, "I've got to admit, getting my parents' approval was a piece of cake."

"You're a lucky one, Arjun," Aditya chuckled in light hearted jest. "I mostly got my parents' approval because I let them know you were going to join us."

Arjun seamlessly changed the subject, concentrating on the final touches. "All right, I've reviewed our list. Is there anything else you guys think we might have forgotten for our trek?"

"Don't worry, I've packed all the energy bars and a stash of dry, instant food items," Aditya comforted. "Well, we learned about that from our previous conversation."

"Along with our clothes, tents, and basics, we've got mosquito repellent, flashlights with batteries, a multipurpose knife, and a matchbox," Arjun summarised.

"Plus, don't forget at least 3–4 pairs of socks, a balaclava, and, of course, sunscreen," Aditya added to the checklist.

Arjun chimed in with a thought: "How about a raincoat? Do we need to bring one?"

"Typically, this season is dry, so a raincoat may not be necessary," Aditya speculated. "But if we have room, it wouldn't hurt to bring one just in case." Aditya's focus altered, and he reached out to their third friend, "Akash, are you still with us? Arjun and I appear to be the only candidates for this exhilaration."

"Come on, Akash, don't let a breakup ruin the journey," Arjun teased. "We're going to have a great time—let go of the past."

"It's not that simple, guys," Akash acknowledged over the phone in hushed tones. "I truly believed she was the one."

Akash's physical build matched Arjun's, a feature that reflected their shared experiences.

"Life evolves, man," Aditya comforted. "She's off to further her education abroad, and long-distance relationships aren't easy. Move on."

"Absolutely, your story with her is already over," Arjun added.

"I didn't expect her to call it quits on the last day of school," Akash said, his voice shaking.

"For now, set her aside and think about this incredible adventure," Aditya said. "Remember, you're the one who put it all together; don't let a breakup ruin everything."

"True," Arjun added with a wry smile. "There are countless heartbreaks out there waiting to rain on our parade."

The ensuing rush of laughter temporarily lightened Akash's load. As their chat gently healed Akash's pain, the trio retired for the night, looking forward to a fresh day full of adventure.

The next day, Akash and Arjun arrived at Aditya's residence, where their adventure was about to start. Aditya opened the door as they rang the doorbell.

"Drop your luggage here, and proceed directly to the dining room table," Aditya said. "My mom has made breakfast for us."

Akash and Arjun set their luggage down a little distance from the shoe rack before proceeding to the dining room table.

"Maa, they're here!" shouted Aditya in the background. He then said to his friends, "You guys start; I'll just get ready and be back in 5 minutes."

Soon after Akash and Arjun had silently seated themselves at the table, Aditya's mother came out of the kitchen carrying a bowl of puris. "It's been a while since the two of you visited," she remarked. "Your expressions reveal the strain of the final exams."

"Yes, Aunty, we're delighted it's finally over," Arjun said with a nod.

Turning her attention to Akash, Aditya's mother inquired, "Akash, you seem a bit quiet. I've never seen you this reserved before."

Akash retorted, "No, aunty, everything's fine. It's just the aftereffect of the exams; we're looking forward to enjoying it now."

Reassured, Aditya's mother said, "That's understandable. Have a fantastic trip, but remember to drive cautiously in the hilly areas."

As they were served puri and sabzi, Akash and Arjun said, "Yes, aunty," acknowledging her counsel.

Aditya eventually joined them at the table, and his mother encouraged him by saying, "Come on and eat with your friends." Aditya agreed and took his spot among the others. After everything was settled, his mother served him puri and sabzi before retreating back to the kitchen.

Arjun leaned down close to Aditya and whispered, "I'm still amazed your dad agreed to let us use the car. How did you manage to persuade him?"

"After my 18th birthday, he's been giving me more freedom," Aditya explained. "I've had my licence for 2 years and have been driving for a while. When I told him about our trek intentions last night, I recommended renting a car for the journey to Dharchula. He surprised me by offering his car. He remarked that I'm maturing and must accept responsibility for my acts."

Arjun agreed, "That's reasonable."

"Lucky, he left for work already; otherwise, he would've given us a lecture now," Aditya added. "He also identified a friend of his at Dharchula, where we might leave the car and start our journey."

"That works perfectly," Arjun replied, "and it saves us the money we'd spend on renting."

"What's with you?" Aditya asked Akash, "Still hung up on that? Just so you know, the journey is 14 hours long, and I won't be the only one driving."

"Yeah, I'm fine," Akash replied. "Don't worry; I'll drive. It will take some time to get back to normal."

Arjun said, "Sounds fair."

Aditya's mother's voice resonated from the kitchen: "If you need more puris, just let me know. Don't be shy."

Aditya turned to Akash and Arjun, asking, "Do you guys want anything else, more puris or sabzi?" Akash declined, saying, "No, I'm good." Arjun followed suit: "Yeah, I'm full too."

A second call from Aditya came, echoing through the dining area: "Maa, we're all set."

Aditya's mother appeared from the kitchen, carrying three little bowls of sugar-topped curd. She explained, "Having curd and sugar is always a good omen before embarking on a journey."

"Thank you, aunty," Akash and Arjun said at the same time.

Arjun signalled Aditya over with a nod as she retired to the kitchen. "Bro, I guess you know, I can't have dairy," Arjun said as he leaned in closer. "Will you help me here?"

"Don't worry, I remember," Aditya reassured. "I'll take care of it."

After finishing their breakfast, the group prepared for their upcoming journey. Before leaving, Aditya paid his respects by touching his mother's feet, a gesture that Akash and Arjun imitated. Farewells were said, and Aditya's mother added, "Remember to call me once you reach Uncle Rawat's home." Aditya nodded and said, "Sure."

As they neared their car, their journey began. The engine roared to life as their luggage was carefully packed in the back. Aditya took the wheel, Akash sat in the front passenger seat, and Arjun sat in the back. Although he couldn't drive, this limitation served Arjun well on this particular trip. His job was to map the route and provide regular advice while they travelled to Dharchula. "Let's roll," Aditya said as he pressed the accelerator.

As they continued on their drive, they turned on the stereo, filling the car with the strains of their favourite songs. Akash was carrying his camera, meticulously recording every detail of their adventure.

Arjun proposed a new venture, stating, "Hey, why not try vlogging? It's quite popular these days."

With a shake of his head, Akash answered, "No, that's not really my thing. I simply enjoy taking photos and videos that we may look back on later. I'll probably put all of the clips together into one video and add some calming music."

"Just a touch of commentary, and voila!" Arjun countered. "It's a video blog. You could even start your own YouTube channel. Who knows, it might take off, and you'll start making money from it."

"I'll pass on that, bro," Akash chuckled, "I'm fine, but thanks for the idea."

After around 2 and a half hours, they decided to take a break in Rishikesh. They parked their car near a café and decided to eat lunch.

Aditya asked Akash, "You holding up okay?" as they placed their orders.

"Yeah, I think so," Akash said.

"Can we take a look at what you've captured?" Arjun asked, seizing the opportunity.

"Not right now; I'd rather not drain my batteries," Akash said. "You can look at it when we get to the hotel."

"All right," Arjun said, nodding in accord.

Aditya said, anticipating their evening activities, "Have we sorted out our accommodation for tonight? I'd rather not drive after dark."

"Yes, I've been scanning the map for suitable lodges," Arjun said. "I believe we might spend the night in Rudraprayag or Karnaprayag. They're roughly halfway along our itinerary, and I've found some beautiful lodges in Karnaprayag."

"Sounds good," Aditya agreed. "We should get there by 7:30 p.m."

Arjun and Akash both nodded in agreement. They began eating as soon as their requested food arrived.

Arjun proposed during a discussion of the evening's choices, "Should we wait here to witness the Ganga Aarti in the evening?"

"I had that in mind as well, but we can't stay here for too long; it'll delay us," Aditya said. "Furthermore, traffic becomes congested in the evening. Perhaps we can spend the day here on our way back."

Arjun asked Akash for his opinion, and he agreed, "Yes, that's a good plan."

Arjun and Aditya wished for Akash to enjoy the journey as much as they did, despite his mainly quiet demeanour throughout. They understood the value of giving him the time he needed to heal and adjust rather than rushing him into something. Nonetheless, they were always involving him. They walked briefly after finishing their meal before continuing on their journey.

"You're driving now," Aditya said as he handed Akash the car keys. "It's my turn to relax."

Aditya grabbed control of Akash's camera as their journey resumed, acting as the photographer in his place. Akash wore a happy look as he sat back in the driver's seat. His eyes remained fixed on the path in front of him with a delicate sparkle. His chosen songs were playing on the stereo, creating a relaxing atmosphere for the journey.

"It's a great sensation to get behind the wheel again after such a long break," Akash added. "Aditya is actually to thank for this opportunity; without his encouragement, I would not have been able to learn to drive. I'm truly grateful."

They exchanged smiles, their camaraderie evident.

"It would've been even better if this blockhead had also learned," Aditya said. "We could have taken turns, making things easier for everyone."

Arjun laughed and said, "Oh, no way. I'm not going to jeopardise your father's car again. I felt so bad the last time; I vowed to learn to drive when I get my own car."

"Don't worry; those things happen while learning," Aditya reassured. "You were only getting started."

"Did your dad scold you for that incident?" Arjun questioned. "Well, yeah, he did," Aditya admitted, "But I'm used to it. He chastises me for a variety of reasons; it's become a habit."

Akash's conversation brought renewed buoyancy to the group's mood. They were enthralled by the music, which was matched by the stunning views of Uttarakhand. Aditya took advantage of every opportunity to take images and videos, but most importantly, he immortalised Akash's radiant smile as they travelled. It's a special thrill to cheer up your buddies and make them feel their best.

As the wheels gently glided along the winding road, a soothing calmness settled over the boys, caressing them like a soft embrace. The picturesque hilly landscape unfolded before their eyes, a masterpiece of nature's artistry. The air, tinged with a hint of earthiness and freshness, flowed through the open windows, carrying with it a gentle breeze that caressed their skin. The rhythmic hum of the engine blended harmoniously with the sounds of nature, birds chirping, leaves rustling, and distant cascading waterfalls, forming a symphony of serenity. They made the decision to stop for a little break in Srinagar after another 2 hours of driving.

Arjun remained in the car as Akash and Aditya went in search of restrooms. Arjun stayed engrossed, his gaze fixed on his phone, as he searched for acceptable hotel possibilities. After a quarter-hour, they returned with three earthen pots of tea and a selection of chips. Arjun pulled himself out of the car, and the three of them savoured the crisp chips while sipping tea from their clay pots.

After finishing their tea, they returned to the car, when Aditya inquired, "Would you like me to drive?"

"No need," Akash replied. "I can manage the driving today."

Aditya responded with a smile, and they all returned to the car.

Akash took the wheel, as the sun approached the horizon, creating a mesmerising show of flaming oranges, rich crimsons, and gentle pinks that blended into the landscape.

The clear clarity of the winter air added to the developing sight, emphasising the grandeur of the surroundings. The hills provided a beautiful backdrop with stark, leafless trees. The low angle of the sun produced extended shadows across the undulating ground, adding depth and complexity.

As they continued on their journey, the sun gradually set below the horizon, immersing their surroundings in darkness. Streetlights appeared and became the only source of illumination visible through car windows. They turned on their car lights and continued their journey, with Aditya happily seated in the front seat and Akash's focus fixed on the road. Meanwhile, Arjun continued to swipe through his phone, looking for suitable accommodations.

They arrived in Karnaprayag to find a busy road, indicating that it was tourist season. After parking their car outside a lodge, they went inside to check about room availability, but their attempts were futile. A similar scenario unfolded when they visited two more adjacent lodgings. Because winter is a popular time for visitors to explore these locations, hotels were in high demand. Resuming their hunt, they returned to their car and drove a little further before finding a good parking spot.

After a determined hour of work, they were able to acquire a single room with three beds at Hotel River View. They retired to their room after parking at the hotel. The exhaustion from the lengthy travel had set in, pushing them to order room service for dinner. Dinner arrived shortly after they had freshened themselves and informed their families of their safe arrival, and they eagerly devoured everything. As the dinner came to a conclusion, exhaustion surrounded them, and one by one, they fell asleep, their bodies yielding to the embrace of slumber.

The next day, at 6 in the morning, Arjun awoke from his sleep and went out onto the balcony. He then put on a warm jacket over a jumper because of the chill in the air before going outside. Fighting the chill, he made his way past the hotel to take in the stunning sunrise view of the valley and the Alaknanda River. He looked for roadside tea stands in search of warmth and was fortunate to find one directly across the street. He took a sip of the steaming tea, which gave him much-needed heat.

His phone rang, and Akash was on the other end as he enjoyed his tea and the scenery. The voice of Akash asked on the phone, "Where are you?"

As an answer, Arjun said on the phone, "Just outside the hotel, taking a stroll and having some tea."

"Okay, wrap up and return soon; we're leaving in half an hour," said Akash.

"Okay, I'll be back in 5 minutes," Arjun guaranteed.

Arjun quickly made his way back to the hotel after finishing his tea. When he walked into their room, he saw that Aditya had already showered and was getting ready to depart.

"Where's Akash?" inquired Arjun.

"He's in the bathroom," Aditya retorted.

Arjun asked, “How long was I out there?” in a state of shock.

“We were awakened when you departed and shut the door,” Aditya retorted with a smile. “When Akash called you, I started getting ready for the shower, and he followed soon after. He ought to be finished in 5 minutes, so get ready as well. We’re going to have breakfast close by and then leave.”

Arjun agreed, “Sure thing. There’s a nice dhaba I saw; the aroma of the food was incredible. We should definitely check it out. We can leave the car here, enjoy our breakfast, and then return before hitting the road.”

Aditya concurred, “Sounds like a plan.”

In due time, they all readied themselves, had breakfast, checked out of their hotel, and made their way to the hotel parking area.

Aditya turned to Akash, inquiring, “Can I take over driving now?” Akash replied, “Of course.” With everyone settled into the car, they resumed their journey.

Arjun, who was seated in the back, instantly started looking at his phone as their journey began to take shape. “We have to travel 260 km today, so the trip should take 8 to 9 hours,” he said. “Both of you will have lots of chances to drive.”

Aditya focused on the road as Akash grabbed his camera and immersed himself in taking pictures of the beautiful surroundings they were passing. They decided to stop in Bageshwar after 3 hours of nonstop travel. They first sought solace in the restrooms, then relished a tea and food break.

They quickly resumed their journey because they still had a long way to go. Akash excitedly accepted Aditya's invitation to drive this time when he inquired whether he was up for it.

Akash continued to drive for another 3 hours before deciding to stop for lunch. They aggressively sought out a decent restaurant after crossing the Ramganga Bridge and quickly discovered one. They decided to take an hour-long break there to discover and photograph Thal's beauties. They later went back to their car.

However, this time Akash requested Aditya: "Bro, could you take over for the rest of the journey?" He was feeling sleepy from his lunch. "I should not have consumed so much rice because I am now really drowsy."

Aditya immediately agreed and said, "Sure thing. Why don't you take a seat in the back? And Arjun can join me in the front passenger seat so he can help me with the route."

Akash calmly sat in the back seat as Arjun nodded his head in agreement and sat in the front.

The scenery progressively became cloudy as they travelled further. Aditya turned on the headlights and changed the speed according to the weather. Akash was on the verge of falling asleep. Arjun successfully navigated the path while also taking advantage of the chance to take pictures of the surroundings with both his phone and Akash's camera. The area was soon completely covered in dense fog as the day grew shorter. They eventually arrived at Uncle Rawat's house after a three-hour drive that went on for an additional hour.

Chapter 2:

Guest's Arrival

Akash awoke from his snooze as Aditya carefully parked the car in front of Uncle Rawat's house. A man who was obviously anticipating their arrival was Mr. Rawat, as he emerged from his house. A retired military soldier named Ashwin Rawat stood strong, his countenance bearing witness to the struggles of life and the stories they weaved together. His skin revealed the story of nature's caress, and his face, carved with lines, bore the history of hours spent in the sun under an open sky. Although his appearance could suggest a severe demeanour, Aditya was well aware of Mr. Rawat's innate calmness.

He remarked, "Ah, here they are, finally arriving. I was just on the phone with your mother." He addressed Aditya and continued, "I'll give her a call to let her know of your safe arrival."

Aditya replied, "Thank you, Uncle. I'll be calling her myself, so I'll inform her as well."

Rawat suggested, "Let's get your luggage out of the trunk."

Akash chimed in, "Thank you, Uncle. Let me assist you. Arjun, can you manage the tent and mat?"

Arjun responded with an affirmative "Of course."

Aditya secured the car, and they entered the house. Mr. Rawat directed, "Feel free to place your luggage in the spacious room I've prepared for the three of you. Given that your aunt and Diya are in Delhi, I had to make all the arrangements."

Aditya inquired, "A sudden trip to Delhi?" To which Rawat explained, "Yes, Diya is participating in an interschool chess championship, and the final rounds are taking place there. She's currently in the semi-finals, scheduled for tomorrow."

Aditya responded, "That's quite exciting. We're all rooting for her victory."

Rawat thanked them and considered, "I'm sure you must be feeling cold. Let me prepare some hot soup for you."

Aditya expressed his appreciation: "Thank you, that would be wonderful."

While they were having this conversation, Aditya noticed Akash and Arjun standing uncomfortably in a corner, realising he had forgotten to introduce them. In order to correct this, he said, "Uncle, let me introduce my friends, Akash and Arjun. We went to the same school together."

"Yes, your father has already told me about them," Rawat acknowledged. He warmly welcomed Akash and Arjun, turning towards them and stating, "Please consider yourselves at home here and don't hesitate to ask for anything you require."

Akash and Arjun uttered the same words of appreciation: "Thank you, Uncle."

All three of them enjoyed the warmth of a shower, one by one, after having driven through the chilly mountain air. They returned to the living room feeling revitalised and refreshed to see that Rawat Uncle had kindly prepared hot soups for them. The soup was bursting with vegetables and smelled faintly of butter.

Akash praised, "Uncle, this soup is truly delightful," as they enjoyed their soup.

"Indeed, these are a few dishes that I can do on my own," Rawat retorted. "I'd have to rely on your aunt and Gobind otherwise."

"Who's Gobind?" wondered Arjun inquisitively.

"Gobind is our housekeeper and cook," said Rawat. "He's coming back soon to make dinner." After receiving a nod from Arjun, Rawat added, "Now, you can all relax. When dinner is ready, I'll call you over so we can talk about what you have planned for tomorrow."

Aditya said, "Sounds good."

The group then went to their assigned room. After making phone calls to their loved ones, they put their phones on charging, and Akash also attached his camera to charging.

They got into their beds and gave themselves permission to take a restorative power nap.

After an hour of restful naps, all three boys stirred awake and heard Uncle Rawat engaged in a conversation with someone. Aditya ventured into the living room and discovered that Rawat Uncle was talking to his father. Upon seeing Aditya, Rawat Uncle gestured towards the phone and said on the phone, "He's awake now; would you like to talk to him?" He then turned to Aditya and conveyed, "Your father wants to speak with you," passing the phone over to him.

On the call, Aditya said, "Hello Baba, everything's fine here… Yes, Akash and Arjun are also up. We're set to start tomorrow morning and might lose signal from then on. Rawat Uncle will keep you updated. Alright, bye," and then ended the call.

Rawat Uncle inquired, "So, all set for tomorrow?"

Aditya responded enthusiastically, "Absolutely."

Akash and Arjun joined them in the living room, seating themselves on the sofa beside Aditya.

Rawat Uncle continued the conversation, asking the trio, "So, the Moksh Parvat base camp trek, huh? What motivated you to choose this particular trek?"

Arjun replied, "We planned for a trek right after our board exams. Initially, we considered Kedarkantha, but there won't be much snow now. We were looking for an intermediate-level trek and explored several options. However, the images from the Moksh Parvat base camp trek truly captivated us. Hence, we settled on this one."

Rawat Uncle chimed in, "That's a good choice. But I must caution you that this trek can get quite challenging at certain points. I've arranged a guide for you; he's a friend of Gobind's and will accompany you throughout the journey. The return from the trek is often tougher due to a long snowy slope at the back of the mountain."

Aditya expressed gratitude, saying, "Alright, that will be very helpful."

Rawat continued, "And do you have all your trekking gear with you?"

Aditya confirmed, "Yes, we've got most of the necessary equipment. We've even practiced setting up a tent."

Rawat replied approvingly, "Excellent. Tomorrow, I'll drop you off at Jalpa, where you'll meet your guide. He'll lead you along the trail. I believe you'll be staying at Surka village on the first day."

Aditya thanked him, and Arjun added, "That sounds wonderful."

From the living room, Rawat Uncle called out, "Gobind, is dinner ready?"

Gobind peeked out from the kitchen and responded, "Yes, sir, it's ready. Should I serve it now?"

Rawat turned to the boys and asked, "Are you all ready to eat?" The boys exchanged glances, and Aditya replied, "Yes, absolutely," as the others nodded in agreement.

After finishing their dinner, the three boys gathered around the fireplace to soak up its warmth and engaged in a brief conversation about their plans for the upcoming day. Gobind had already departed after serving dinner, and Mr. Rawat was in his room conversing with his wife over the phone. This continued for a little while before the boys rose from their seats, acknowledging that an early morning awaited them.

As they made their way towards their room, Rawat Uncle emerged from his own quarters, remarking, "I apologise for the delay; I was speaking with your aunt."

Aditya responded reassuringly, "No worries; I hope she's doing well."

Rawat Uncle confirmed, "Yes, everything's fine on their end. Diya has already retired for the night; she's got a big day ahead, just like you guys." The boys exchanged smiles and glanced at each other. Rawat Uncle carried on, "So, off to bed, are you?"

Akash replied, "Indeed, we need to rise early tomorrow, so it's wise to get some rest now."

Rawat Uncle nodded and offered, "Alright then, don't hesitate to ask if you need anything. Good night." With that, he retreated to his room, and the boys did the same, heading to their own quarters.

The following morning, Uncle Rawat rapped on their door at around 5:30 a.m., announcing, "Boys, are you up? It's already 5:30 a.m., and we need to be on the road by 6:30."

Arjun, still wrapped in the tendrils of sleep, stretched and rubbed his eyes, then shuffled to the door, unlocking it. He mumbled, "Yes, uncle, I'll wake them up." Returning to the room, Arjun gently nudged Akash and Aditya until they were roused from their slumber. He then ventured to the bathroom to brush his teeth and take a shower. Upon Arjun's return, both Akash and Aditya were in line, with Aditya next to use the facilities.

Akash inquired, "How are you feeling, Arjun?" to which Arjun replied, "Excited and a bit nervous."

Akash wondered, "Nervous? Why?"

Arjun explained, "Well, it was relatively easy from Dehradun to here, but the true adventure begins today. I've never been on a trek before. At least you two have some trekking experience."

Akash assured him, "Don't worry, you'll do just fine."

Arjun nodded and instructed Akash, "Alright, go ahead for your shower. I need to call home."

In another 40 minutes, the trio was ready, clad in their trekking attire and equipped with their gear. Gobind had also arrived early, preparing a hearty breakfast for all. Following the meal, the boys loaded their bags into the car's trunk. Mr. Rawat informed them that his car had some battery issues, so he would drive them in Aditya's father's car and later pick them up from Jalpa once they returned from the trek. Mr. Rawat took the driver's seat, with Aditya beside him in the front, while Akash and Arjun occupied the back.

Mr. Rawat stated, "I believe it's about 30 kilometres from here, which should take around an hour and a half."

Aditya acknowledged, "Okay."

The car took a moment to start; the engine was sluggish due to the cold, but after 15 minutes of persistence, it roared to life.

As the vehicle ascended further into the hills, a sense of elevation pervaded the air. The world below appeared remote and trivial, while a feeling of expansiveness settled within them. Sunlight filtered through the forest canopy, casting intricate patterns onto the road. The stillness, interrupted only by distant natural sounds, enveloped the car in a cocoon of tranquillity. It was a precious escape from the usual daily clamour—a chance to detach, unplug, and simply be immersed in the present moment. Minds once cluttered with thoughts and concerns now seek refuge in the simplicity of the drive. No words were exchanged during the journey, just the serenity of sitting, observing, and being lost in the peace. After about an hour and a half, they reached Jalpa.

Upon the car's arrival at a tea stall, a sturdy and youthful lad of about 21, with patchy facial hair and a build that reflected the rugged strength of a typical mountain resident, approached Mr. Rawat. He inquired, "Mr. Gobind sent you, right?"

Mr. Rawat confirmed, "Yes, and who might you be?"

The man introduced himself, saying, "I'm Sharad, your guide."

Mr. Rawat responded, "Ah, excellent."

With everyone exiting the car, the boys exchanged greetings with Sharad and introduced themselves.

Mr. Rawat inquired, "Are there any formalities to complete here?"

Sharad explained, "Yes, I've already filled out the forms. We just need your ID proofs and Rs. 200 for the official formalities at the checkpoint," he said, nodding towards the boys.

From his wallet, Mr. Rawat produced two Rs. 100 notes, passing them to Sharad. He commented, "Here you go."

Aditya interjected, "Uncle, please, we have enough cash; there's no need for you to pay him."

Rawat responded, "It's alright. Just hand him your IDs." Aditya relented, providing his ID card to Sharad first, followed by Akash and Arjun.

After collecting the IDs, Sharad instructed, "You can all sit here," indicating the tea stall, "and I'll be back in 30 minutes."

Aditya asked, "Uncle, would you like some tea?"

Rawat replied, "Certainly, a cup of tea is always welcome in the cold." Aditya extended the offer to Akash and Arjun, receiving nods in return. Aditya ordered the tea vendor, "Uncle, 4 teas, please," and handed the tea seller a Rs. 50 note.

Immediately, Mr. Rawat stood up, asserting, "No, no, you can't pay. Why should you pay when I'm here?"

Aditya insisted, "Please, uncle, you've already paid Sharad. Let me handle this."

Mr. Rawat responded, "No, you can cover it for me when you start earning. For now, allow me this pleasure."

Aditya tucked away his Rs. 50 note. Side by side, Aditya and Mr. Rawat savoured their tea, while Akash and Arjun ambled nearby, enjoying their own cups. After roughly 30 minutes, Sharad returned with their IDs.

Mr. Rawat questioned him anxiously about the trek's specific itinerary, to which Sharad, the sturdy mountain guide, replied with a confident smile. "Allow me to lay out the itinerary for you," he said. "We're going on a four-day trip. The first two days will consist of a moderate uphill trek, with the second day spent pitching our tents for the night at the base camp. The third day is all about reaching the breathtaking viewpoint before returning to base camp. Finally, on the fourth day, we'll return here. Surka, a 5-kilometre hike away, is our target today. Through Surka's trail, we will go to the base camp tomorrow. Fortunately, we've arranged for comfortable homestays in Surka for tonight's rest." This comprehensive explanation garnered nods of understanding from Mr. Rawat.

Turning to the trio of enthusiastic young trekkers, Mr. Rawat inquired with a touch of paternal concern, "Are you all mentally and physically prepared for the adventure that lies ahead?"

The trio, Aditya, Akash, and Arjun, exchanged glances charged with determination and responded collectively, "Absolutely, sir! We're up for the challenge!"

Mr. Rawat turned his focus back to Sharad and gave him one last directive, delivering it with a hint of sternness. "Please, Sharad, look after these youngsters well. Although they may be enthusiastic, they lack experience. Make sure they stay together at all times, and keep a close eye on them. Priority one is safety."

Sharad, a young man with a stern demeanour, firmly nodded as he accepted the duty. "I'm here for you, sir."

With parting smiles and farewells, Mr. Rawat and the trio exchanged goodbyes, and Sharad stepped into his role as the guide. Guiding them along a narrow, winding path through the verdant jungle, he shared insights about the surrounding flora and fauna, offering an occasional glance back to ensure his charges were keeping up.

In the meantime, Mr. Rawat started his car, the quiet hum of the engine blending in with the noises of the mountains. He took a quick peek at the trail, which was now hidden by the thick undergrowth, and then started back, certain that the three young, intrepid travellers were in good hands as they set off on their trekking quest.

Chapter 3:

Conquering the Incline

The boys made their way across the mountain's difficult terrain with the help of their reliable hiking poles. Although it was a narrow trail, it took them along the mountain's edge and occasionally past patches of lush vegetation. Only the mellow melodies of nature's orchestra—the melodic voices of birds and the delicate whispers of the wind—broke the general atmosphere of peaceful tranquillity. Amid this tranquil backdrop, a soothing tranquillity enveloped them, offering a welcome sanctuary from the cacophony of daily life. This symphony of noises appeared to be created by nature itself, which contributed to its distinct aspects. A beautiful audio tapestry was created by the interplay of the soft rustling of leaves, a far-off waterfall's crescendo, and a nearby stream's murmuring. But what really got the guys' attention was how effortlessly Sharad moved along the route. He moved fluidly, keeping up a steady pace, pausing now and again to make room for the boys, who periodically trailed a little.

After an hour of walking, their enjoyment of the trip started to wane, leaving their legs worn out. Arjun broke the awkward silence by asking, “Could we perhaps take a short break? I’m feeling quite worn out.” Arjun had never had to carry a heavy rucksack across a mountain before, so the effort was starting to become apparent.

Sharad agreed with his request and said, “Of course, sir. Let’s take a 10-minute break.”

They settled in after locating a perch on a nearby boulder. Aditya questioned, “How much distance have we covered?” interested in their progress.

“We’ve travelled about a kilometre,” Sharad retorted. “There are still roughly 4 kilometres to go.”

Arjun cried out in a mixture of shock and horror, “What? Just one kilometre? Even after a continuous hour of walking?”

“Yes, sir,” Sharad said. “In the highlands, distances can be deceivingly slow to traverse.” Their once-excited faces now showed a mix of sadness and the mounting weight of tiredness.

Sharad stood to his feet after 10 minutes and said, “Let’s move on. If we choose to stop for lunch, we still have roughly 1.5 kilometres to go in the next 2 hours.”

Arjun was curious: “Where are we stopping for lunch?”

“There is a store on the way,” Sharad retorted. “You can find some refreshments there.”

In agreement with the answer, Arjun nodded. They stood up and got ready to leave once again. Noticing Arjun's fatigue, Sharad walked behind him and adjusted his backpack, asking, "Feeling better now?"

Arjun retorted, "Much better, thanks," with gratitude, "Now it's much more comfy."

Akash and Aditya were also given guidance by Sharad, who urged them to "Make sure your bags are properly adjusted as well." They heeded his advice and fastened their backpacks. Sharad also suggested, "Don't take your baggage off while you sit or rest. Later, it will be more difficult to carry them."

They put their luggage on and continued on their way. Akash retrieved his camera out of his bag and started recording their journey as he started to feel more at ease. He held conversations with each of them and recorded their comments as he questioned them about their opinions of the trek. He even turned to Sharad and asked him about his background and his stay in this industry. They travelled another 2 kilometres while having these discussions.

Their destination came into view. A modest store made of wood and aluminium sheets, with food packages hanging outside, came into view. They exhaled in relief as they carefully set their luggage down on the grassy area next to the store, their shoulders temporarily becoming lighter. Arjun entered the store to look at the available meal options, but there weren't many.

"There isn't much diversity here," he said upon returning. "Maggi, eggs, bread, and a few other snacks are available."

Akash added, "I'll have Maggi and an omelette."

Then Aditya said, "Same for me."

"I was thinking of having the same," Arjun continued. "Let me ask Sharad if he wants something."

To find Sharad, he went around the back of the store and inquired, "Sharad, what would you like to eat?"

"There's no need to order for me, sir," Sharad informed him. "It's my friend's store here. Just place your orders, and I'll get something for myself."

Arjun agreed, saying, "Okay if you say so."

After placing the order, he joined his friends again. Akash used the opportunity to record some images and videos. He relished the comfort of being able to walk without having to lug around his luggage. Akash joined the party for lunch once omelettes and sizzling platters of Maggi had arrived. The Maggi had a peculiar flavour that was infused with the scents of garlic and coriander, giving it an unusual but delectable flavour. After eating, they took another 15 minutes to relax before continuing their journey.

The gradient steadily got steeper as they continued on the trek. As a result, they moved more slowly, but they persisted. Their luggage's weight started to press again on their shoulders. The temperature was slowly dropping, and the area was shrouded in fog. With each step, Sharad warned them to be cautious because the fog was getting thicker. Surprisingly, Sharad continued to travel with ease, pausing whenever the boys fell behind. He carried a smaller bag than the lads, which contained only necessities as well as a down jacket.

The boys were aching for a break after an hour and a half of walking. Sharad suggested, realising that they were all tired, "Let's continue for another 10 minutes, and then there's a suitable spot for you all to rest." The boys persisted through those extra 10 minutes, their steps sluggish from exhaustion. They eventually arrived at a wide area with few trees that looked more like a field than an open space. A run-down house with damaged windows stood in a corner of the region. They eagerly dropped their bags as they sat on the steps next to the house. They struggled to follow Sharad's advice to not take their luggage off because their shoulders ached.

While they were resting, Arjun asked Sharad, "What is the history of this place?"

Sharad responded, pointing to the home, "An elderly man used to live there many years ago. One of the oldest residents of the village, he liked a quiet life and opted to live apart from Surka. After his death, the mansion was abandoned. It progressively fell into decay due to a lack of maintenance."

Akash continued frivolously, "It looks quite eerie, like a haunted house."

In response, Sharad said, "True, it may seem that way, but it isn't. Numerous people go past this house through these hills, but none have ever seen anything unusual. In reality, I stop here occasionally on my way to Surka. It's a tranquil retreat, in my opinion."

They remained seated and experienced the same sereneness that Sharad had mentioned, engrossed in a few minutes of silence. Their exhaustion was relieved by the serene atmosphere created by the mist-covered surroundings and the soft caress of the chilly breeze. The tranquillity was further enhanced by the way the leaves on the trees moved gently in response to the wind.

They took a refreshing 15-minute break before getting up. The boys followed Sharad up the trail while carrying their backpacks on their shoulders. They travelled on through the lush forest and along the sides of the mountain. They stopped for a brief 10-minute break whenever tiredness set in. They had to go for another 3 hours before reaching Surka village. Only 20 to 25 stone and wooden houses with clay-tiled roofs made up this small village. As they neared their destination, their exhaustion appeared to lessen. They were supposed to spend the night at their assigned homestay, which Sharad escorted them to.

He indicated a nearby house and added, "You can stow your luggage in the room and then come over here." He continued, "There's a source of warmth and comfort inside," giving a welcoming glance at the adjacent house. "Additionally, we have some soup and tea that will lift your spirits."

The three immediately placed their baggage in the corner of their room after entering. Three single beds, each covered with a blanket, were located in the room. Akash and Aditya quickly took off their shoes and took care of their personal hygiene, while Arjun, who was visibly affected by the plummeting external temperature, hastily sprawled onto a bed and cocooned himself under some covers. The area was already completely dark. Arjun's trembling form remained on the bed as Akash and Aditya prepared to enter the residence as instructed by Sharad. Akash inquired, "We're heading to that house, as Sharad suggested. What about you?"

Arjun responded, "You guys, go ahead; I'll join you later. This cold is too much for me."

As soon as Akash and Aditya left, Arjun was left alone.

Sharad entered their room after over an hour and said, "Sir, you must go to the other room with the fireplace; otherwise, you'll keep feeling cold."

Arjun was on the verge of falling asleep when Sharad prompted him to get up. "Yes, I'll be there shortly," he murmured.

Sharad only gave a quick glance to make sure they had enough blankets before leaving. Even after donning every jacket and jumper he had brought on the trip, Arjun still felt the need for warmth. He mustered the will to get up despite the chill, wrapped himself in a blanket, and went to the next-door residence.

He was surprised by an unexpected sight as he entered the room: his buddies were mingling amicably with strangers. A woman in her fifties and a man in his thirties were occupying the space, and their faces obviously displayed their knowledge of coping with the difficulties of extreme cold and bore the distinctive signs of natives. There was also Sharad. Aditya and Akash enjoyed their soups while relaxing on a seat with their feet in warm water. The woman quickly handed Arjun a bowl of soup once he settled down next to them.

Arjun playfully nudged Aditya, querying, "Why didn't you call me earlier? This room is incredibly warm and comforting."

"We were so comfortable that we thought you'd join us eventually," Aditya responded.

"Could you direct me to some warm water so I can soak my feet?" asked Arjun.

Promptly, the lady presented him with a basin of warm water, along with an encouraging remark, "Here you go; also try this ginger-infused soup for a revitalising effect. Let me know if you need more."

Arjun responded, "Thank you, ma'am."

"This is my uncle, who is overseeing the homestay business here," Sharad said as he presented the new faces to Arjun. "And this is my grandma."

Arjun greeted both people politely and shared a smile. The warmth of the room enveloped the group, making their weariness and exhaustion seem to vanish. "Dinner would be ready in approximately an hour," Sharad told them. "Make yourself at home here by the fireside until then."

After an hour, as the boys received plates of rice, lentils, and veggies for dinner, a wave of relief swept over them. Their only sources of food all day had been snacks, protein bars, and Maggi. They went back to their room after supper. They had to give in to sleep because of their weariness after the day's journey. They struggled to get comfortable on the frigid mattress and wrap themselves in the chilly blankets since the bedding felt icy on their bodies. They eventually found some comfort in their own body heat, making the conditions tolerable until they fell asleep.

The next morning, the boys were roused from their sleep by a soft knock on the door and Sharad's voice. "Sir, kindly get up. We have to start by 8, and it's almost 7 o'clock," he told them.

The guys roused themselves in response to the appeal. Surprisingly, they experienced neither pain nor fatigue—typically associated with treks—instead, they felt invigorated with a fresh vigour. The first to go was Akash, who opened the door to a beautiful view that briefly rendered him speechless. The village's real beauty had stayed hidden, as the previous evening had been covered in darkness when they had first arrived. He invited Aditya and Arjun to join him and take in the breathtaking view, but he quickly withdrew indoors because of the bitter cold. Akash went back outside after wearing his jacket and went to the adjacent room to ask the old lady for some hot water for the group. They took a warm bath to relax and prepare for breakfast, following the same procedure as the day before. They gathered in the adjacent room for breakfast after taking baths, feeling refreshed and renewed.

After enjoying roti and sabzi, they slung their backpacks over their shoulders and started their journey. As they prepared for the day's travel, Aditya paid the woman's bills and bade her farewell. Soon after, Sharad showed up, dressed in his trekking attire and toting a bigger rucksack this time. He had a little gas cylinder with a cooker attached that he carried along for cooking.

"Will we need crampons for walking on snow?" Aditya questioned.

"Yes, as there will be snow beyond the base camp," Sharad affirmed. "Tomorrow, you can wear them."

They set up their equipment and started moving forward.

They started on the next phase of their adventure, making their way through a treacherous jungle for an hour before coming out into a broad clearing. They were already about 17,000 feet above sea level due to elevation, and the trees grew sparser as they went higher. Compared to the previous day's trip, today's challenge of covering a distance of 7 kilometres was more difficult because the terrain was steeper and more rocky. Surprisingly, the boys had travelled for close to 2 hours without stopping. They had to take off their jackets because of the warmth that came from the sun rising overhead. When exhaustion took its toll, their progress was interspersed by brief stops, after which they would muster the energy to carry on. Aditya once again filled in for Akash, who was carrying the greater duty as a photographer and videographer. They arrived at the specified rest area, a wooden house with thatched roofs, after travelling for another 4 hours. Sharad made hot water and boiled the noodles the lads had packed, which would serve as their immediate nutrition for the following 2 days, as they sat down on the bench inside. They had already travelled more than 4 kilometres when they became satisfied and took a quick break. Sharad estimated they would reach the base camp by 6 o'clock in the evening.

When they started again, the surroundings became obscured by an engulfing fog. A continuous hour of walking revealed Akash's uneasiness. "I don't feel good, guys." He worried that it might be acidity or something.

Sharad quickly replied, "Alright, take a seat here and drink some water," pointing Akash to a nearby rock where he could perch. "Do any of you have antacids?" he inquired as he turned to face the others.

Akash received the necessary antacid from Arjun when he took out a tiny envelope from his luggage. After 5 minutes of taking the medication, Akash felt relieved. "Are you feeling better?" Sharad asked, "Ready to move forward?" Akash gave a nod of agreement.

The three found themselves again giving in to exhaustion as they continued on their quest, their pace dropping. "Come on, boys, we need to pick up the pace," urged Sharad, who was keen to keep them moving. "It will be challenging to get to the camp once it gets dark. The future's route also becomes dangerous."

Strangely, their hurried efforts only appeared to make them more weary. Their sight was reduced to just 10 metres by the thick fog, which obscured their view. "All right, folks, we're about to traverse the ridge of the mountain," Sharad said after a while. "Be extremely cautious. Although there won't be much of an elevation difference, the stretch is hazardous. Follow closely behind me as I lead."

The boys were really worn out, but they had a deadline to meet. Akash was particularly straining; his breath was laboured as he dragged along. They carried on their march under the direction of Sharad. During their journey, conversation was a lifeline, especially when they were periodically unable to see one another due to the dense fog. It was necessary to march in a single file due to the restricted path. Sharad kept watch, making sure no one fell behind.

Suddenly, Arjun asked Aditya to check the back of his neck as they continued: "Aditya, could you help me? It is quite itchy."

Aditya replied, "Yes," while examining a red, inflamed spot that was probably the result of a bug bite.

They continued their walk after Aditya applied an ointment he had taken from Arjun's backpack. After that, Aditya asked Akash, "Akash, do you have any water? Mine is finished."

Adding his own, Arjun said, "Mine is too."

But there was clearly no answer from Akash.

Alarmed, Aditya raised his voice: "Akash? Where are you?"

Correcting Aditya, Arjun interjected, "Why are you shouting in that direction? Akash was in front of me."

Aditya insisted, "No, he was behind me. I heard his steps just a few minutes ago."

Arjun's tone turned anxious. "Akash? Where are you?"

Aditya, raising his voice once more, called out to Sharad, "Is Akash with you?"

Sharad promptly replied, "No, he's not with me. What's the matter?"

Aditya conveyed their dilemma: "We've lost track of Akash. Could you come here, please?"

Sharad, his anxiety palpable, hurried towards them, asking, "What happened?"

Aditya explained, "We can't locate Akash. Can you assist us?"

A panicked Sharad inquired, "Oh my god, where did he go? Wasn't he walking with all of you?" Arjun confirmed, "Yes, he was with us. We turned to ask him about water, but he didn't respond."

With a sense of urgency, Sharad determined, "Let me check if he's lagging behind somewhere. Stay put; I'll return soon." He retraced his steps along the narrow trail and, within moments, was swallowed by the enveloping fog. Aditya and Arjun called out for Akash repeatedly; their calls were met only with eerie silence.

About 15 minutes later, Sharad returned in a hurry, having ventured back to the beginning of the ridge in search of Akash, yet to no avail. Arjun's question, "Did he fall off the ridge?" cast a shadow of concern. The colour drained from Aditya's face as the possibility sank in. Sharad's heart raced in terror upon hearing the question. His eyes widened and his face contorted with sheer panic, his heart pounding like a wild stallion's hooves.

"Wait here again; don't move," he urged, before dashing back to the trail.

A quarter of an hour later, he returned, his face marked with frustration, saying, "I carefully scoured the area again, but the dense fog makes visibility almost impossible. I called his name but received no response."

Both Aditya's and Arjun's eyes welled up with tears, their minds grappling with the unsettling reality of the situation. Sharad seemed utterly bewildered and at a loss for what to do. Arjun, on the brink of tears, implored, "This can't be happening. We can't lose Akash. We have to find him."

Sharad, his voice weary, responded, "I understand your urgency, but searching in this dense fog, with darkness falling, is an insurmountable challenge. It's getting harder to see by the minute."

In Sharad's thoughts, a chilling realisation crept in: If Akash had slipped down the ridge, the odds of survival were slim. Yet Sharad recognised that lingering here would imperil everyone, given the encroaching darkness. In a fragile moment, Sharad regained his composure and explained, "I comprehend how difficult this is, but right now, I must ensure your safety. With light fading and temperatures plummeting rapidly, we're in grave danger here. We need to move forward and find a safe spot to set up camp. We may not reach the base camp, but we have to move."

Aditya's voice rang out, filled with desperation: "We can't just leave Akash behind. He's our friend."

Tears streamed down his face. Arjun echoed Aditya's sentiment, resolutely saying, "We can't abandon him."

Sharad, trying to soothe their agony, implored, "I get it, but we can't continue searching now. I need to ensure your safety. Please come with me. Tomorrow morning, we'll return and search for Akash."

Aditya's sobs intensified, with a plea in his voice: "Please, we can't leave him like this." Sharad, almost pleading, responded, "Please, sir, understand. The longer we stay, the darker it gets. Staying could cost us all our lives. Come with me."

Aditya and Arjun, overcome with sorrow, stood up, their sobs punctuating their movements. They picked up their bags and followed Sharad. Walking behind them, he urged them to move faster, guiding them onward as darkness continued to descend. After 45 minutes of sombre progress, they reached the end of the ridge.

"Retrieve your headlamps and turn them on," Sharad instructed, his own torch casting a faint glow. "We have another 30-minute walk to a safer camping spot, less exposed to the wind."

Guided by their torches, they pressed on, grief and fatigue weighing them down. Silent determination propelled them forward; words seemed futile. It remained surreal to them that Akash wasn't with them. Eventually, they reached their destination, where Sharad assembled his tent with their help, the torches illuminating their efforts. Although the tent was snug for three, they accommodated themselves inside, physically and emotionally drained. Their personal tent, which they had brought with them, went missing along with Akash. Once the tent was set up, Sharad collected branches for a campfire.

As flames flickered to life, he inquired, "Would you like to have dinner now?"

Arjun's voice held a monotone quality: "I'm not hungry."

Aditya concurred, "Neither am I," and they retreated into the tent to rest.

Sharad understood their grief, but the weight of his own helplessness was a burden he couldn't share. He attempted to use his phone, hoping for a network to call for assistance, but 'no network' was the disappointing result. Despite his extensive trekking experience, this situation was unprecedented. Since the boys didn't eat, Sharad too entered the tent without supper. Gradually, even the campfire's glow subsided, leaving them enveloped in darkness.

Chapter 4:

Hunting for a Companion

In the middle of the night, within the confines of the tent, Arjun nudged Aditya gently and murmured, "Are you awake?"

Aditya's whispered response was, "Yes, I can't sleep."

Arjun, matching the hushed tone, echoed, "Yeah, me neither."

Aditya shared his sentiments: "I still can't wrap my mind around the fact that Akash is no longer with us."

Arjun's whisper carried a mix of hope and uncertainty: "I know, but I have this lingering feeling that he might still be alive. It's as if we should be out there searching for him."

Aditya's voice retained its softness: "I'm grappling with the same thoughts. Yet, we have to consider Sharad's perspective: searching in the dead of night would be perilous. The darkness is complete, and even the moonlight can't pierce through the cloud cover."

Arjun's next words came as a quiet suggestion: "I've been thinking, what if we sneak out around 3 AM? By that time, there might be some faint light breaking through, especially once we reach that ridge. Besides, the frigid cold is another factor. Akash may not endure it for long."

Aditya weighed in with a nod, saying, "You have a point. Sharad won't permit us to venture out before sunrise, and he's right about the risks. Sneaking out before he's awake seems like the only option."

Arjun agreed, "Absolutely, we should attempt it while he's still asleep." The exchange of whispered ideas continued until 3 AM, at which point they finalised their plan to cautiously slip out and begin their search.

Aditya carefully got up, trying not to awaken Sharad, and slowly opened the corner of the tent. He silently got out, followed by Arjun. They used their mobile screens' dim light to take out and carry only the essentials with them. Once they were suited up, they slowly started walking. After they were at an adequate distance from the tent, they turned on their headlamps and headed towards the ridge.

It was extremely scary for them to wander over the mountains at such late hours in the darkness, but they had their best friend's life at stake. There wasn't as much fog as there was earlier, but it was windy and extremely cold. Even though they were wearing all of their warm clothes, they were still shivering. They kept walking in the dark, holding each other's hands, and not talking much.

At one point, they were confused about which path to take because they were not sure and stood still. Arjun, after thinking for 5 minutes, pointed at one of the paths, and they took a chance to go through that way. Luckily, after walking for another 20 minutes, they found the ridge. The trail looked more dangerous than before. They slowly started walking over the ridge, and they knew they had to walk a long path before they reached the point where they lost Akash. They had walked for almost an hour on the trail when they found a piece of a white wireless earbud.

Aditya said, "I think that's mine; let me check," and he picked up the earbud and added, "Yup, it's mine; this scratch formed when I dropped it last week."

Arjun replied, "I think we were sitting here when we lost Akash. Let's sit here for some more time, and when the light comes, we can proceed."

The fog had receded a lot. They flashed their headlamps towards each side of the ridge to check if they could find something. They sat there for another 30 minutes when a part of the sky started glowing, but that was not enough for them to see. They had to wait another 30 minutes until everything was somewhat visible.

Aditya and Arjun continued flashing lights to check if they had any clues. They walked forward and backward on the ridge to make sure they didn't miss anywhere. Aditya noticed that on the left side of the ridge, some damaged, dry bushes caught his eye. He called Arjun immediately, and they both flashed their lights around those bushes.

Aditya said, “Those bushes seem to have been damaged recently, as if something big might have fallen off. I guess that’s our clue.”

Arjun said, “Don’t you think it will be dangerous to reach there? What if we fall down?”

Aditya replied, “We have to take this risk; if Akash is there, we have to save him.”

The sun was above the horizon now. They gingerly attempted to descend the ridge, positioning themselves with their backs against the soil and securing their feet in the mountain soil. They grasped onto the dry bushes atop the slope for support. Patches of snow dotted some areas, adding an extra layer of caution to their descent. Slowly and meticulously, they navigated their way downward, all the while being mindful of the presence of snow.

Sharad awoke on the other side of this endeavour, feeling shocked. When he realised that both Aditya and Arjun were missing, even though their possessions were still in the tent, he felt a wave of terror. His thoughts were filled with uncertainty, and he was unsure of what to do. He hastily scanned all directions in an effort to find them. He shouted their names, but he received no answer to his calls. The seriousness of the circumstances suddenly dawned on him. He quickly checked his phone for a network connection out of a sudden sense of urgency, but to his disappointment, there was none. He remembered a place nearby that would give him the required signal and realised he needed to find a location with better reception. He quickly moved in the direction of that location, driven by the urge to get assistance.

Aditya and Arjun searched the area thoroughly as they went down the mountain and arrived at the location of the damaged bushes. Their gaze was drawn to a phone, and following closer study, they determined that it belonged to Akash. It had a tenuous lifeline, with barely 4% of the battery remaining. Looking down, they tried to figure out what path Akash might have taken during his fall. Arjun continuously cried out Akash's name in a frantic attempt, but their echoes were met with stillness.

They pressed on, determined not to forsake their companion, pushing farther down in their search. After a few hours of hard work, they arrived at the bottom of the slope, in front of a river stream designated by the emergence of a narrow waterfall's crest. Recognising the opportunity to replenish their water bottles, they placed their bags carefully in a dry spot and cleaned their faces and hands. Despite the fact that fatigue was tugging at them, they pressed on, not allowing fatigue to derail their objective. A low growling sound disrupted their surroundings as they replenished their water supply and drank the refreshingly chilled water.

"Did you hear that?" Aditya spoke quietly.

"Yes, I heard it as well," Arjun responded quietly. "Are you thinking the same thing I am?"

"It sounds like there might be a bear nearby," Aditya said.

"Stay still; it might not have spotted us." Arjun directed Aditya's attention to the source of the noise.

"I see it," he muttered, "right near the waterfall's crest. It hasn't yet noticed us. Let us keep our cool."

They realised they might have to flee if the bear noticed them. "We should collect some stones; maybe we can scare it off," Aditya offered. As Arjun proceeded to gather stones, his copper water bottle fell, causing an unintended clang.

Their hearts beat faster as they turned to observe the bear's reaction. To their horror, the bear had already focused its gaze on them and was approaching. Because of Aditya's quick thinking, they decided to run alongside the stream. The youngsters continued their hurried retreat, negotiating hazardous, rocky terrain as the bear raced forward and crossed the creek. They were forced to ascend after being cornered, but the rocks were slick due to melting snow. Fear gripped them as the beast got closer. They prepared themselves for an approaching attack, convinced that their fate was determined.

The bear attacked with astonishing speed, causing the boys to close their eyes tightly in horror, ready for the blow. A transient azure brightness pierced their sealed eyelids in those seconds of fear and gloom. As Aditya slowly reopened his eyes, he saw the bear flee, leaving him both surprised and perplexed. Aditya shifted his gaze to Arjun, who sat hunched like a ball, his eyes closed in prayer. He called to him, “Arjun, get up; it’s gone.” Arjun remained seated in the same position, his ears blocked, praying and shouting fervently. Aditya reached out and tapped Arjun’s shoulder, causing him to scream even louder.

Aditya, frustrated, shouted, “Hey! Relax, it’s gone.”

Arjun stopped screaming and opened his eyes, asking, “Is it really gone? Did you try anything to get it to go away? What occurred?”

Aditya replied, “I don’t know, something happened; I just had a brief glimpse of the bear leaving.”

Arjun expressed his gratitude, saying, “Oh, thank you, Bholenath; you saved us. Thank you very much.”

“I sensed something was here, something that might have scared the bear away,” Aditya reflected. “Let me take a look around.”

Aditya looked in every direction, including scrutinising the cliff above, but discovered nothing out of the ordinary.

“Regardless of what it was, we’re safe now,” Arjun said. “We must proceed with greater caution. I’m not sure what happened to Akash.”

“All right, we should keep moving,” Aditya urged. “There doesn’t appear to be any way forward in this direction; therefore, we’ll have to descend by the waterfall.”

“All right,” Arjun said.

With unwavering determination, Aditya and Arjun pressed on in their search, descending the mountain with calculated care. The terrain gradually shifted, leading them into a more forest area. As they descended, their eyes keenly scanned their surroundings, and amidst the foliage, they noticed a piece of fabric caught on the branch of a bush. Their hearts quickened as they investigated further, realising that it was a fragment torn from Akash's muffler. The discovery affirmed their path, strengthening their resolve.

Their descent led them to fairly take notice of a strange formation within the mountain—a natural cave-like structure. Arjun was inspired by the thought of this refuge and suggested, "Perhaps we should explore that area; it could serve as a safe haven." As they made their way back down the mountain, they came across a stream that they suspected came from the waterfall's bed. After crossing it, they ascended once again, arriving at the spot they had seen from afar.

Their bewilderment intensified as their eyes took in the scene before them. Akash's stuff, including his luggage and clothes, was neatly stacked. Drawing nearer, disbelief mingled with relief. Akash was nestled amid his belongings, cocooned within the folds of his garments and the tent. Their activities were fuelled by a sense of urgency. Aditya, an aspiring doctor, used his medical skills to put his fingers on Akash's forehead, and then his neck, assessing his temperature and pulse.

Together, they determined that Akash was dozing off with comfortingly regular breathing. They gave their sleeping pal a gentle prod and called out his name in an effort to wake him. Akash, though, remained constrained by his sleep. In an effort to rouse Akash, Arjun quickly uncapped his water bottle, sending a cascade of drops all over his face. His eyelids began to twitch open gradually, showing their beloved friend's sleepy yet awake gaze.

Chapter 5:

An Uninvited Guest

Time slipped by a little as Akash gradually recovered consciousness and his confused mind began to make sense of the world. An overpowering wave of emotion overcame him as realisation sank in, and he fiercely hugged his friends as tears streamed down their faces. Aditya and Arjun's friendship with Akash was reinforced by this emotional reunion, and neither of them could control their own tears. Aditya said, "Take it easy, buddy," with a trembling voice. The knowledge that they had successfully located Akash, unharmed, was a colossal victory that reverberated strongly within them.

After the initial flood of emotions subsided, Aditya extended his hand to help Akash sit, their fingers interlocking in a show of solidarity. Arjun, his curiosity piqued, posed the question that lingered in their minds: "Can you recall how you ended up here? What happened yesterday?"

Akash's response was a struggle, his voice marked by difficulty as he admitted, "I'm not entirely sure; my memories are fragmented."

Aditya's mind raced, sceptical that Akash could have simply fallen off the mountain and ended up in this location. Arjun concurred with a thoughtful nod.

Even with his voice straining, Akash slowly described his ordeal: "Bits and pieces are coming back to me. Last night, I woke up in a completely different location: beneath the ridge, perched precariously on the edge of a cliff, and covered in dense foliage. My entire body was in pain; the fall had left its mark. I must have passed out while strolling alongside you two. I could make out the hazy contours of the moonlit landscape as my eyes adjusted to the darkness. I was in pain, but I was able to sit up. As a sombre reminder of the peril I was in, I could see the rocky valley below me. I tried to call out your names out of desperation, but my voice betrayed me." He added, "My meagre attempts were abruptly silenced by a roaring sound that resonated. I scanned the area in an effort to identify the noise's origin. The unpleasant realisation that someone was coming up behind me was what came next. I struggled to turn around, and the sight that greeted me terrified me."

Arjun pressed, "What did you see?" as his interest grew.

"Two dazzling eyes came from the darkness and drew closer with each step," Akash recalled, his voice still laced with residual anxiety. "I was able to make out the face of a powerful snow leopard as the moonlight showed more of it. The beast closed the gap with a methodical approach that appeared almost purposeful. I forced myself to stand despite my terror because I knew that any movement would send me plummeting into the abyss. The leopard quickened its pace as it sensed my mounting panic, culminating in a quick leap in my direction. I closed my eyes in resignation to my fate as I was overcome by fear. The imminent collision was followed by total darkness."

"When I woke up just now and saw you both, it was a relief beyond words," he continued after taking a breath. "What led you to me?"

The measured Aditya said, "We'll explain as we ascend."

"Agreed, our current top priority is to return," Arjun said.

"Sharad must be in a panic now that he's realised we're not in the tent. It is indeed already daylight," Aditya said as he nodded and noted the passing of time. "Most likely, it's between 9:00 and 10:00 AM." He looked at his watch, which corroborated Arjun's estimation that it was exactly 9:52.

Akash took Aditya's hand and rose to his feet with unexpected ease, filled with resolve and fresh optimism. He said with a joyful realisation, "Remarkable! I can't believe I'm no longer in pain. My elbows, back, and legs all appear to be in excellent condition."

Arjun and Aditya exchanged perplexed looks as they tried to make sense of this sudden turn of events. "While we could be ignorant of your recent recovery, the good news is that we must return before Sharad organises a search squad," Aditya said with a wry smile.

Akash nodded resolutely in agreement, saying, "You're right; let's move on."

The group then started climbing, their ascent being marked by their friendship and unwavering resolve to find Sharad and overcome the obstacles in their way.

As they arrived at a location that bore a resemblance to the initial point of the waterfall's brink, Aditya's voice resonated with determination: "We need to traverse this stream and proceed in that direction," gesturing towards the east.

Seizing the opportunity, Aditya recounted the recent episode to Akash: "You'll scarcely believe what happened here a couple of hours ago. We were pursued by a bear during our search for you. But remarkably, something occurred, and the bear abruptly retreated."

Akash's curiosity was piqued, prompting him to inquire, "What exactly do you mean by 'something happened'? Can you explain?"

Aditya confessed, "To be frank, I'm not entirely sure. I perceived the bear lunging at us and reflexively shut my eyes. The next instant, upon reopening them, I observed the bear's hasty departure. I distinctly recall glimpsing a brief flash of blue light as I regained my vision."

Akash's memories appeared to link the events: "A blue burst of light? That's fascinating. Now that you mention it, I did experience a similar blue light yesterday when the snow leopard attacked me before I passed out. Isn't that a strange coincidence?"

Aditya said, "Your situation is equally puzzling," acknowledging his confusion. "After all, to find that cave, we had to first climb down the mountain, and then ascend. Do you think the snow leopard may have carried you there while arranging your clothing as a temporary blanket?"

Arjun jokingly said, "Perhaps the leopard wasn't hungry at the time and intended it as a cosy nest for later." Their laughter erupted.

"It would be terribly disheartening not to find its bundle intact," Aditya added, grinning.

Akash expressed his concerns amid the jovial banter, saying, "There's something genuinely confusing happening amid the humour. I fell over a cliff and suffered injuries, but I awoke completely healed, while you both managed to avoid being harmed by the bear. Everything is very strange."

"This isn't the same route we took," Arjun said, realising what he was saying. "The environment is strange here."

Aditya agreed, saying, "You're right, even though we initially took what seemed to be the right course."

Arjun nodded, assuring himself, "Yes, that's what I thought as well."

"Look around; is there anything we can use as a reference to find our way back?" Aditya asked, analysing their surroundings.

"In this dense forest, the odds of finding such a reference are slim," Arjun replied. "Our first aim should be to locate a passage back to the ridge's crest."

"Agreed," Akash said, "let's focus on that."

"All right," Aditya said.

"Once we're back atop the ridge," Arjun reasoned, "We can hopefully orient ourselves and determine the correct direction." "Alright," Akash and Aditya agreed, nodding.

Their hunt for the summit continued as they climbed further towards the top of the mountain. Sharad's worries were taking over as he pondered the seriousness of the situation as it developed. He was able to get a phone signal once he arrived at a particular spot, allowing him to make a call for help. He quickly returned to the campground he had created by retracing his steps. Friends from Surka were on their way to help, and it seemed likely that they would arrive in the evening. With few choices, he made the decision to keep looking until they arrived. He meticulously combed the area, searching every crevice, before moving forward towards the ridge.

On the other side, the trio of friends resumed their trek up the mountain through winding trails and rocky outcroppings, their laughter and joke-telling fostering a spirit of friendship. It was as though they had temporarily forgotten the difficulties of the previous day. They found a minute to relax whenever fatigue set in, munching on supplies they had brought with them. While traversing the mountain, they even went fruit picking. Despite the cheerful atmosphere, Akash seemed thoughtful.

When Aditya noticed Akash's expression, he asked, "Are you still thinking about last night's events, Akash?"

Akash reacted to this by saying, "It's just so bizarre; waking up healed overnight."

However, Arjun seemed to approach the discussion with humour, asking Akash, "Were you really hurt, or perhaps you were having a really vivid dream? Did you inadvertently smoke something on the walk?"

Akash became defensive in response to the taunting and asked, "Are you out of your mind? Everything I told you was real!"

Arjun said, "Alright, maybe you're getting superpowers like Wolverine," in a cool tone. "You simply recover more slowly."

Their banter continued throughout the day until they arrived at what appeared to be the top of the hill. The landscape was sparsely forested, with patches of snow. The realisation that they had spent the entire day getting to this point dawned on them as the sunlight faded into dusk.

"Can you guys recognise anything about this place?" Akash said, as they were lost in their foreign surroundings.

"I have no recollection of yesterday. The fog made it impossible to see anything clearly," Aditya acknowledged, "so I'm as clueless as you."

"Does anyone have an active phone?" Arjun inquired. "GPS or a compass could be useful. My phone's battery is dead."

Unfortunately, none of their phones were working. The predicament got worse.

With a sudden surge of optimism, Arjun started to shout out for their missing guide, "Sharad," as though the mountains would carry his voice. When there was silence, Aditya and Akash looked at each other. "Worth a shot," Arjun agreed.

"We ought to choose a nice camping location before dusk comes," Aditya said. They were on an uneven level, and Arjun warned that strong winds could make camping in such regions dangerous. "There's a chance that our tent won't hold up, and thunderstorms pose a lightning risk."

"I noticed a forested area below," Akash said. "There's a location that would be suitable for camping."

"It seems like our best option for the moment," Aditya concurred.

They made their way back to the forested region and arrived at a clearing that, while gently sloping, offered ample space for erecting their tent. The area was enveloped by towering trees and a carpet of small bushes. As Akash began the process of unpacking his bag and assembling the tent, Aditya and Arjun gave him a hand to set up the camp. Despite the day's adventures, the prevailing warmth had kept the chill at bay, yet as the darkness deepened, the temperature took a plunge, leaving the boys shivering.

As the sun gave way to impending darkness, Aditya's concern was evident as he remarked, "It's growing colder, and the darkness is setting in. We need to set up the campfire to keep warm. Let's gather as many branches as we can."

Arjun, understanding the urgency, replied, "Alright, I'll work on gathering more firewood. You go ahead and start the fire."

Aditya, realising the essential component was missing, inquired, "Okay, can you pass me the matchstick?"

To his disappointment, Arjun responded, "I thought you had lit it up yesterday. I didn't bring any matches."

Frustration tinged Aditya's voice as he exclaimed, "Oh, come on!"

Curious about the exchange, Arjun inquired, "What's wrong?"

Aditya sighed as he realised, "I left the matches in my bag, in Sharad's tent."

Arjun's response was concerned: "Oh no." His tone became more urgent as he added, "We won't survive the cold without a campfire."

Aditya tried to reassure Arjun, saying, "Calm down; we'll find a solution. Perhaps we can try a 'Man vs. Wild' scenario, starting a fire with a knife and a pebble. Let's look for a smooth pebble; Akash should be carrying a knife."

They swiftly searched their surroundings and were fortunate to find an appropriate stone that would be useful for their attempt to start a fire. "Akash, do you happen to have a knife in your bag?" Aditya spoke as they approached their campground, interrupting the silence.

"Yeah, let me check," Akash said as he stepped out of the tent after spending time assembling the shelter. He dug about in his baggage with a sense of purpose, pulling out the knife and asking, "What do you need it for?"

"We need it to ignite the fire," Arjun retorted urgently, "as someone accidentally left the matches in his bag."

"Hold on a second," Akash said quickly. There was a brief pause before he resumed his quest, evidently intent on finding what was required.

Aditya and Arjun's thoughts turned to the difficulty of starting a fire with the knife as well as the upcoming conflict. Then, unexpectedly, Akash intervened with a solution, offering them a lighter and saying, "Here you go."

"You have a lighter?" Arjun exclaimed as he reacted with a mix of amazement and bewilderment. "Why didn't you bring this up sooner?"

The truthful reply from Akash was, "I honestly didn't know you needed it."

"Hold on!" Aditya continued his inquiry after his curiosity had been aroused. "Why do you even have a lighter at all? Have you been smoking?"

After a brief moment of hesitation, Akash said, "Well, to be honest, I bought a few cigarettes and thought of smoking, but I don't think I need them anymore." Arjun added a supportive comment, saying, "That's a wise choice."

"Remember, we're here to help you," Aditya said in a soothing tone. "Just try to stay away from such things."

"Yes, you're correct," Akash continued. "It was only a passing occurrence. Now, I'm doing better."

"All right guys, it's getting darker," Arjun said, taking the initiative. He replied, "I'll go gather more branches," and he set off to gather more firewood.

Akash withdrew into the tent while Aditya began the job of building the campfire, arranging the adjacent branches for the purpose. Aditya used the opportunity as he lit the campfire to have a meaningful talk with Akash. "Akash, how are you feeling?" he inquired. "You must have experienced a lot during the past few days."

As he replied, Akash's voice came from within the tent, reflecting on his most recent experiences. "You know, it's hard to put into words. These last three days have taught me something very important. This life is far bigger than our individual conflicts. We frequently find ourselves reflecting on unimportant details and our uncontrollable history. However, it opens up new facets of living when we turn our attention to the present and the future. It highlights the value of looking out for and spending time with the people who matter to us. If it weren't for you people, I'm not even sure whether I would be alive today. To save mine, you both put your lives in danger. There is no way I could imagine something better than that. Thank you so much for being a part of my life, both of you."

Akash's sentiments were acknowledged by Aditya with a smile, and they both fell silent. While this was happening, Arjun came back to the scene with a sizeable amount of branches and twigs for the campfire.

As a sign of his exhaustion, Arjun said, "Okay, I'm extremely exhausted right now. Any suggestions for our meal?"

Akash offered a solution after coming out of the tent, stating, "I have some protein bars and a collection of wild fruits we collected on the trip. Unfortunately, there is no water left."

Aditya came up with a solution right away, saying, "Well, we can melt some snow. Please give me your copper bottle, Akash. I'll put snow inside."

From his luggage, Akash took out his water bottle and handed it to Aditya. Akash and Arjun sat down in front of the bonfire and basked in its warmth as the day faded and the surroundings grew darker. Aditya, meanwhile, took advantage of the chance to gather clean snow and carefully fill Akash's water bottle. They hung the bottle above the bonfire by tying it to a stick. The contents of the bottle warmed up over time, giving them a way to quench their thirst. Some of the water was also used to clean the wild fruits that they planned to eat. Despite its meagre satisfaction, their improvised dinner was all they had. They limited their stay outside because they were aware of the rapidly dropping temperature. The once-large bonfire progressively shrank in size. Fortunately, the tent provided cover for the group, though it was not impervious to the freezing temperatures.

The guys shivered uncontrollably as the temperature dropped. They realised night had really fallen as darkness encompassed their surroundings.

"Akash, do you have anything else we can use to keep warm?" Arjun wondered. "It's getting too cold to bear."

"No, just my clothes," Akash said, "although..."

He stopped for a moment, causing Arjun to ask, "Although what? Go ahead, shoot."

"I do have something that might help you stay warm," Akash continued.

Arjun, curious, inquired, "What is it?"

Akash stood up on his knees and began looking for something. Perplexed, Aditya inquired, "What's going on?"

"Please wait a minute," Akash begged.

Akash used his torch to find a small bottle holding a crimson liquid. Aditya responded immediately, exclaiming, "Seriously?"

"What?" Akash defended himself. "Because of the cold, I carried it. A little of this should warm you up."

Arjun admitted, hesitantly, "I've never consumed alcohol before."

"Given how you're shivering, this will give you much-needed warmth," Akash reasoned.

Aditya added, "I can't really endorse this, but I have read that mixing rum with warm water can help raise body temperature."

Arjun sighed and reflected, "I suppose I don't have much choice then."

The group left the tent after making a choice. Aditya attempted to rekindle the campfire with the remaining branches as Akash held the torch. Meanwhile, Arjun used the water bottle to gather snow from the area. They heated the bottle over the fire once more, this time getting it to a marginally higher temperature. They arrived at a comfortable temperature after letting it cool down a bit. They poured a measure of rum after the contents of the bottle were heated enough, each taking a careful taste. Although it wasn't much, it was enough to have a warming effect and promote sleep. "Let's keep this between us," Arjun said after giving the subject some thought. "I'm in serious trouble if my parents find out."

Akash and Aditya exchanged knowing smiles. They put their temporary fix in place and allowed the bonfire to gradually go out before retiring to the tent for the night. Sleep soon overcame them.

Around 3.30 AM, Arjun was roused from his slumber by a cacophony echoing outside their tent. He was groggy and unsure whether the noise was genuine or a fabrication of his imagination. He prodded his sleeping buddies, intending to rouse them, but their rest was undisturbed. He struggled with a mixture of anxiety and urgency as he gradually became conscious of his bladder's urgent demands. He summoned the strength to call out to his buddies, only to discover them lost in their dreams and his vision engulfed in pitch-black darkness. He fumbled for Akash's torch; his need was pressing. He resolved to go out alone, fuelled by rising desperation.

Arjun arose from his prone position with measured resolution and delicately unzipped the tent flap, each metallic clink echoing in the night. As he faced the abyss beyond, the shudder in his bones reflected the quiver in his heart. Arjun flourished the torch, its glow dispersing the shadows like mist, despite the moon's gentle shine casting a weak luminosity across the terrain. His quest for a good resting location brought him to a dense underbrush thicket snuggled to the side. He set out with a deep breath and a whispered prayer.

Arjun tended to his urgent need in the engulfing darkness, shielding the flashlight's beam to conserve battery power. After completing his mission, he began his return journey, only for his steps to falter. Two small orbs hovering in the abyss held an unearthly glow in the darkness. Arjun's thoughts recoiled in astonishment as he imagined the phantom. These iridescent orbs hovered in the distance, like phantom lamps in the abyss, approaching him with disturbing grace.

Terror ran through his veins, yet his survival instinct propelled him forward. He retraced his steps, a whispered mantra of self-assurance keeping the terror at bay. He recalled that he had the flashlight tucked away in his pocket. He retrieved the flashlight with practiced speed and, with quivering hands, shone its bright light at the approaching spectres.

The glowing orbs turned into eyes, which were now merged into the terrifying aspect of a wolf. Its muzzle is an ebony blade with a sinewy elegance that tapers to a pointed tip, evoking an innate grace. Glistening teeth, bathed in the predatory lustre of moonlight, erupted from the wolf's lips, drawn back slightly in a dangerous curl. Arjun recoiled in surprise as a wave of horror raced through him. He dashed to the tent, his scream piercing the night's silence and awakening Akash and Aditya from their rest.

The two boys emerged from their haven, dazed by the suddenness of their awakening and uninformed of their friend's experience. They were greeted by the sight of Arjun, his face drenched in sweat and his eyes ablaze with panic. He was rendered speechless by the tremulous glow of the portable light he clutched. Aditya's inquiry cut through the strained air, a trio of questions attempting to solve the mystery, "Where were you? What happened? Are you alright?" Arjun only pointed at the source of his anxiety, a lupine shape lurking in the darkness.

The wolf's plaintive howl penetrated the silence in that tense moment, echoing with a melancholy tenor. The trio became ensnared by a spreading encirclement, and their senses heightened to the point of fear. Additional pairs of brilliant eyes eventually emerged from the obscurity, punctuating the landscape with their eerie brightness like ethereal sentinels.

The party was encircled by a pack of 7 or 8 such lupine apparitions, their presence a terrifying representation of the unknown.

The trio of young men stood motionless, a look of apprehension on their faces. Akash managed to escape the tent's confines while clutching his bottle securely. Akash's actions were directed by an innate impulse as the wolves advanced at a measured tempo. With a deliberate gesture of intimidation, he tossed his copper bottle at the first of the lupine figures, but the improvised missile barely hit its target. Rather than deterring the animals, the activity seemed to pique their interest, igniting the flames of their rage. The guys immediately crowded closer, their eyes screwed tight, and their palms held in a desperate alliance of shared fear. As their inevitable demise neared, an unexpected intervention occurred.

A shift occurred in the midst of the uncertainty. The scenario had changed when they ventured to reopen their eyes. Three of the once-advancing wolves were now recumbent, their bodies distorted in pain. The boys gradually became aware that some enigmatic power was at work. Before they could fully comprehend the cause of this unusual upheaval, they realised they were not alone. Swift as lightning, an ethereal blue figure appeared, a blur of motion poised against the turbulent night. It caught the incoming attack of wolves with a powerful surge, establishing an impenetrable barrier. The tension in the air appeared to make the air itself quiver.

In an astounding crescendo, a piercing resonance rented the air—an auditory attack with a vehemence that surpassed the bounds of simple sound. The unified howling of the wolves in response showed how successful this operation was. The heart of the advancing pack was punctured by the piercing screech, acting as a deterrent. One by one, the lupine phalanx disappeared into the night, a testament to the enigmatic figure's dominion over their territory.

The guys were captivated, astonishment written across their faces as they tried to make sense of the bizarre picture before them. The once-enigmatic figure, which resembled a human form, had materialised precisely in their line of sight, though its position obscured its face. Its stature exceeded 6 feet, emanating an overwhelming bulkiness, a tribute to its immense strength. Its hands, aglow in a luminous blue that gradually faded, captivated their attention. They deduced from their careful observations that these radiant appendages were the source of the otherworldly illumination. As their initial horror gave way to interest, the shape of the figure's look became clearer—it was dressed like a guy, wearing jeans and a jacket.

Akash gripped the reins of his courage, summoning a sliver of his dormant resolve, and yelled out, his voice punctuating the electrified air, "Excuse me! Who are you?"

The response was a symphony of unknown phonetics, expressed in a deep and gravelly tone that rang with parental authority. The perplexing interaction continued as Akash attempted to bridge the linguistic divide by repeating his question, "Pardon me?"

The figure flipped its position, tilting towards the trio in an unexpected twist. It joined its hands in a respectful gesture, accompanied by a spoken response delivered in a distorted dialect that indicated its foreign origin: "I apologise. Allow me to introduce myself. My name is Mauktik. I hope you three are alright."

The figure's countenance was obscured by shadows, hidden beneath a thick facial mask and the shroud of its jacket's hood. Their attention was drawn only to the dazzling azure brilliance coming from its eyes amid its veiled appearance. Aditya extended a warm salutation, his voice bearing an undertone of thankfulness: "Hello, my name is Aditya, and these are my companions, Akash and Arjun. We want to express our profound gratitude for saving our lives." Akash pressed on, his voice ringing with a mixture of intrigue and astonishment. "Who are you? And how did you get your hands bright? Do you have any extraordinary abilities?"

"As I mentioned, my name is Mauktik," Mauktik responded, his tone measured. "I hail from a realm far beyond this universe, a species known as *Janatig*."

The reality of Mauktik's extraterrestrial identity became clear among the cadence of questions. Aditya, seeking clarification, ventured to express their collective awe: "So, you are an extraterrestrial visitor. What journey brought you to our planet, and what reason has brought you here?"

Simultaneously, Akash began a similar inquiry, his voice full of curiosity: "Where exactly is your home planet located? How large is the space between our worlds? Furthermore, how did you learn of our existence and our planet? Is your presence unique, or do others of your sort inhabit this realm?"

Mauktik's eyes were perplexed as these queries whirled around, even as Arjun absorbed the conversation, his fatigue visible in half-lidded eyelids. A speck of doubt flared within him amid the frenzy of interaction, wondering if reality had been infiltrated by the realm of dreams. The bite of the cold night air awoke him from his drowsiness with the realisation that this was, in fact, a tangible meeting.

Arjun's voice emerged, accentuated with a tremor of cold-induced haste: "Friends, if it's alright, could we perhaps continue our conversation within the confines of the tent? I'm getting rather cold out here."

Mauktik's response was prompt and accommodating: "Of course, please proceed inside."

Aditya inquired about Mauktik's comfort in the frigid temperatures, to which Mauktik responded with tenacity, indicating that the cold was manageable for him. Mauktik remained outdoors, so the trio withdrew to the safety of their tent. Conversation resumed within the warm embrace of shelter, but Mauktik stood guard just outside, keeping an eye on what was going on.

Chapter 6:

Quest of a Stranger

The clock had just struck 4 o'clock in the morning, and the outside world was still cloaked in darkness. The trio found sanctuary under the tent's cosy confines, cocooned in warmth. In stark contrast to this setting, Mauktik sat on a wooden log, a watchful sentinel in the dark. He braced himself for the onslaught of questions ahead.

"Would you mind unveiling your visage?" Akash began the inquisition, his voice politely urgent. "Your face is obscured by the mask and hood."

In his measured answer, Mauktik expressed regret in a deep, manly, sore voice, saying, "I apologise, but such an unveiling is beyond my discretion. I'm on a mission that necessitates caution, not simply about myself but also about the nature of my endeavour."

Aditya asked, "How did you find us in this remote location?" accented by curiosity, through the pale brightness of the night. "What brought you here, exactly?"

"For the past 3 months, I've lingered in these mountain realms, waiting for the arrival of three wanderers whose guidance is crucial to my quest," replied Mauktik, his response laced with a sense of resignation and revealing of his guardedness.

Akash tried to make sense of the situation and asked, "Wait, are you saying that you were looking forward to our arrival?"

The reply from Mauktik was ambiguous, contained a subliminal acknowledgement, and said, "To a certain extent, I guess."

Aditya, a natural inquirer, bridged the gap with another question, his words laced with intrigue: "So, how did you have foreknowledge of our meeting? We set off on a journey, mistakenly deviating from our intended route to come here. Is it possible that your presence influenced our path?"

"No, not quite," Mauktik replied, explaining himself. "I came across your friend last night while climbing the highlands. He was under attack by a leopard, a dangerous circumstance that necessitated my involvement. After ensuring his safety, I transported him to a neighbouring cave in the valley below. When I went out to get some food the next morning, I came across you and your friend in a dangerous encounter with a bear. My quick efforts forced the bear to flee, and I fled quickly to avoid notice. I discovered his disappearance when I returned to the cave, bearing some fruit for your companion. The subsequent search led me to the three of you, an encounter that triggered a sensation of recognition, implying that you might be the people I was looking for."

Akash's realisation rippled across the conversation, illuminating a link: "Ah, that explains the vivid blue flash of light we witnessed."

Mauktik nodded in agreement, validating the deduction.

Aditya, his curiosity unabated, asked another question, his voice tinged with amazement: "So, you mention that you are of extra-terrestrial origin? How do you manage to speak our language so well?"

Mauktik's response was a tapestry of experiences, a portrayal of a one-of-a-kind adventure. "I've been on this planet for about 2 years. My terrestrial adventure began when I landed in the sea near Italy. Since then, my travels have taken me to a variety of locations, culminating in my landing here. I arrived in India around a year ago, beginning a journey through its different landscapes and cultures. This trip gave me the opportunity to immerse myself in the languages of many places. Over the course of my travels, I learned 18 languages, 10 of which were indigenous Indian dialects."

Aditya's response was a simple "Wow" that encapsulated his feelings of adoration and astonishment.

"Here I struggle to secure decent grades in my second and third languages, yet in a span of 2 years, you've mastered 18 languages," Arjun interrupted, his voice laced with a hint of humour. "Perhaps I should have been the one to fall off the ridge."

With a gesture, Akash calmed Arjun before asking another question in an enquiring voice: "Could you explain the manner in which you journeyed to our planet? Furthermore, how big is the space between the two worlds?"

Despite being astounding in scope, Mauktik's statement had a matter-of-fact quality. "From Earth's perspective, the distance is equivalent to almost 750000 trillion light years. However, we utilise cosmic tunnels as a form of transportation, which significantly shortens the route."

Aditya took a risk and asked, "What exactly is a cosmic tunnel?" This was a question that carried the seeds of illumination.

By bridging the verbal and conceptual divide, Mauktik began to explain, saying, "What you could refer to as a 'black hole', we refer to as a cosmic tunnel. This is a massive object with a dense core that warps space-time. A significant rift in the space-time continuum is created within its singularity, which is its core. An instantaneous rip in the fabric of space-time is caused by this indentation, which is produced when mass and energy are absorbed above a particular threshold. This brief opening, which takes place as the puncture appears on the other end of the universe, acts as a bridge or tunnel connecting nearby universes. An enormous amount of energy is released in a burst of gamma rays when the puncture appears in the other universe. We take advantage of this occurrence for our interstellar trip."

Arjun's interest was quickly caught; he was intrigued by the conversation about space, his passion. "So you're suggesting the actual existence of an Einstein-Rosen Bridge?" he said, excited.

"Speak of science, and his inner Einstein comes to life," Akash added with a joking remark and a playful tone.

"Regrettably, I'm not familiar with the specific concept you're referring to," Mauktik apologised to Arjun.

With an unwavering sense of curiosity and a sincere tone of inquiry, Arjun continued his investigation: "Okay, but how can you manage to withstand a black hole's gravitational pull?"

With the attitude of a seasoned professional, Mauktik replied, "We are outfitted with specialised suits meant to interact with the invisible matter within the black hole's event horizon, leaving us impenetrable to its gravitational effects. But we must cut down on the amount of time we spend there. We time our entrance to coincide with the formation of the universal bridge inside the cosmic tunnel to ensure quick passage—entering just after it begins and leaving immediately."

"Tell us about your extraordinary powers," Akash pressed further, diverting his attention to Mauktik's extraordinary abilities. "Where do you get your abilities?"

"Our species inherently possesses these unique capabilities," Mauktik explained succinctly, but with a sense of innate amazement. "As we grow older, we focus our efforts on improving specific abilities."

"My mind is reeling from all of this," Arjun said, expressing his surprise. "Please tell us more about yourself and these amazing revelations."

"As I previously mentioned, there is much I am restrained from revealing, both about myself and the nature of my mission," Mauktik said, returning to caution. "I'm here to fulfil a prophecy, and my presence will end once that prophecy is fulfilled."

Akash said, his tone rising with expectation, "So, what did this prophecy entail?" Akash was driven by a need to comprehend the intricate details of this prophecy. "It predicted our meeting, right?"

With a nod, Mauktik confirmed that Akash's reading was accurate.

Akash inquired further: "What course of events did the prophecy lay out beyond our meeting?"

The way Mauktik responded gave off the impression that his direction had been predetermined: "It specified that you all would lead me to Namah Parvat, a waypoint on my voyage. I am supposed to travel north from there, following indications that would eventually bring me to my predetermined encounter with Brahmarishi."

"Where exactly is this Namah Parvat?" Aditya said, his voice trembling with uncertainty. "I'm not familiar with that name."

"I'm in the same boat," Akash said, echoing Aditya's inquiry. "And who exactly is this Brahmarishi?"

"Are you absolutely certain about the name?" Arjun said, his tone tinged with doubt. "It does not correspond to any of our understandings."

"Indeed, we embarked on a trek bound for the Moksh Parvat base camp," Aditya interrupted again, emphasising their perplexity. "It's possible you mistook our identities for those of others."

Mauktik answered with a resolution that broke through the cloud of uncertainty, demonstrating a depth of insight, "I am aware of the Moksh Parvat, and from what I understand, Namah Parvat is located to the east of that location."

"Alright, whatever this is, we aren't equipped to guide you there," Arjun said, his scepticism still obvious. "The truth is that we have no idea what it is. There's a good chance you've mixed us up with someone else."

Akash's sentiments were similar to Arjun's, with his voice bearing a feeling of finality. "Yes, and given everything that has happened, I believe it would be prudent for us to abandon the journey and return to our homes."

The conversation ebbed and flowed with the passage of time until the sky began to lighten, signalling dawn. The guys' eyelids became heavy with exhaustion after being awake since their meeting with Mauktik. Mauktik, ever vigilant, understood their need for rest, saying with understanding, "You should rest now. We have a long road ahead of us."

Responding to Mauktik's proposal, the boys found themselves on the verge of falling asleep, their faculties exhausted. As Mauktik left, they succumbed to tiredness and fell asleep to recover their energy stores.

After a two-hour nap, the boys awoke to the presence of the sun that had already ascended the sky, indicating that it was likely around 8 a.m. Aditya was the first to emerge from the tent and observed a strange sight in front of them: a cluster of wild fruits skilfully camouflaged beneath leaves. "Mauktik, are you around?" he inquired, breaking the silence.

Mauktik's deep voice rang out from a high position atop a large tree branch; his response was affirmative: "Yes, I am here."

Aditya's eyes were drawn upward as he spoke, his inquisitiveness evident. "Have you been observing us like this since yesterday?"

Mauktik's reaction was straightforward: "More or less."

The remaining two lads soon joined Aditya outside the tent, their combined goal being to rekindle the flame in order to melt ice for drinking water. They packed their stuff and started off on their trip after finishing the wild fruits.

Mauktik descended effortlessly from his perch in the trees, keeping a safe distance as the group set out on their journey.

When they arrived at the peak they had previously visited, confusion muddled their decision. "I believe we should proceed westward, in the direction from which we initially arrived," Akash suggested, making a familiar proposal.

"No, that's the way towards the ridge," Arjun responded, highlighting the uniqueness of their current location. "This terrain is a different one."

"He's right," Aditya said in agreement with Arjun. "The weather was hazy that day, clouding our view of the sun's position after midday. Furthermore, all of our phones have died."

Aditya's voice resonated across the landscape as he pleaded with Mauktik for help. "Do you have knowledge of our correct path, Mauktik?"

Mauktik's faraway voice expressed his apprehension. "I'm afraid not. I intend to follow in your footsteps. I'm hoping that your path coincides with the path to Namah Parvat."

"However, our goal isn't to reach Namah Parvat." Akash's resolve was obvious as he emphasised their aims. "We're going home."

Mauktik remained still, his silence reflecting their announcement. An unexpected sight came from the shadows, advancing from the rear and swerving towards the east, in the middle of their collective perplexity. Arjun, noting the unexpected occurrence, inquired, “Isn’t it rather unusual to encounter a dog in these environs?” as a dog emerged from their back.

“No, I’ve witnessed dogs accompanying travellers throughout the trails, sometimes guiding them along the path,” Akash responded, drawing from a reservoir of experience. “We could try to follow the dog; it might lead us to a nearby village or some type of civilisation. From there, we may possibly contact Sharad.”

“Oh, my goodness! We totally forgot about him” said Aditya, reflecting his awareness. “Sharad must be losing his mind.”

“Let’s not waste time,” Arjun said, his impatience obvious in his tone. “Let’s go with the dog.”

With a sense of purpose, the boys set off on the path guided by the stray dog, trailed by Mauktik, who kept a silent vigil in their wake.

Meanwhile, on a different front, Sharad had sent a distress call to a neighbouring village, pleading for help. Responding to the summons, a few villagers assembled at the indicated place a day earlier, despite the fact that their search efforts had not yet begun. They all set up camp in the same location where Sharad had originally set up shelter for the night. With Sharad in their midst, he continued to offer a detailed narrative of the events as they unfolded, leaving no detail out. With the light of morning illuminating the ground, Sharad and the search party set out to hike down the ridge. Sharad’s demeanour indicated a mixture of anxiety and apprehension, despite his youth and the weight of responsibility for three lives. His emotional distress was apparent, with an incredible powerlessness arising from his inability to comprehend what had happened. He struggled with the harsh reality that no action on his part could have stopped the catastrophe from unfolding. Sharad led the assembled searchers to the precise area where he last witnessed Akash, carving that horrible memory onto the terrain.

A small team of about five guys was poised for action within the search party. "This slope is incredibly steep; should anyone have plummeted down here, the prospects of their survival appear bleak," one of the members said, his tone vibrating with concern. "This path leads to a forested region below with difficult terrain and a flowing waterfall."

"It's been two nights since the boy went missing," a separate person said, his words loaded with gloomy realism. "Even if he survived the fall, the brutal reality is that he could have been killed by the wild residents of these ranges, such as snow leopards and roaming wolf packs. These predators emerge from the darkness driven by the primal need for sustenance and water."

"Nonetheless, our duty is to search for them," Sharad said, steadfast in the face of hardship. "We cannot predict their fate ahead of time. If they're out there in danger, we must do everything we can to find and help them."

A search party member, moved by Sharad's dedication, expressed their preparedness: "Young man, I understand. We will investigate every possible avenue."

A young team member was chosen by the search party to take charge of the situation. One of the men pointed to the chosen one and said, "You, there—descend along this ridge," with a sense of direction in his voice. "You will be held in place by a rope. We want to search both sides of this cliff. It's your job to move downhill and look for any possible traces. If you don't find anything, we'll then descend to the valley and take a different path that leads to the waterfall to look at it from a different angle." Following the plan, the chosen teenager was safely bound with a rope and sent on his mission to look for even the smallest hint.

Meanwhile, the trio persisted in their difficult trek across the barren mountain environment, which was occasionally decorated with patches of snow. They split up Akash's possessions so that each had an equal burden. The dog also kept up a slow, deliberate pace, showing awareness of their position in the rear. They continued their journey for the entire 3 hours, but they could see no indication of any traces of civilisation or human habitation. They clung to the hope of a quick find as they navigated both uphill and downhill terrain. They decided to stop their journey, giving themselves a small respite, realising the need for relief. The canine buddy sat down next to them, reflecting their need for rest. Their food and water supplies were dangerously low, and they were on the verge of running out. It became immediately clear that there were no feasible possibilities for food because there were few trees and dry bushes, making it impossible to collect natural fruits. They distributed the poor array of fruits and protein bars amongst themselves, relying on the little supplies they had obtained at the beginning of their excursion. They offered some to Mauktik, but Mauktik politely declined the offer.

They continued their trek after a half hour break, with the faithful dog accompanying them once more. After another hour of trekking, they saw a huge change: the entire length of their path had been covered in snow.

In light of this transition, Aditya asked a lingering question in their collective minds: "Do any of you have a clear sense of whether we're ascending or descending?"

"Conventional wisdom suggests snow accumulates at higher elevations, but our trajectory appears to lean towards descent," Arjun interjected.

"Fog's rolling in again," Akash said, reflecting their common feeling. "Our best bet is to keep marching. Let us put our trust in this canine buddy and see where it takes us."

Mauktik's presence had now become insignificant; the trio's sole attention was on returning to safety.

As the snowfields spread out in front of them, their pace naturally slowed down, but their footsteps still left a trail in the snow. The temperature continued to drop over the course of the subsequent 3 hours that were spent across the snowy edge of the mountain, which was made worse by the chilly wind gusts. The fog gradually dissipated, revealing a soft golden sunlight that caressed their faces with its warmth. Their progress was abruptly stopped by a presence in front of them as increased clarity and the clearing of the fog both developed simultaneously.

A massive mountain rose up in front of them, beyond the valley, its imposing presence covered in a fresh layer of snow that, in some places, revealed a clear and particular pattern. The summit received the last of the sun's rays as it shed a brilliant orange glow that gave the area an unearthly feel. As they all took in the magnificent sight, time seemed to stop, and a calmness descended across their faces. Their expressions seemed to reflect an unconscious notion that they had never before experienced such peace of mind.

Mauktik, who had remained in the background, moved forward as time seemed to stand still. He gently knelt down ahead of the boys, touching his forehead to the icy floor in a sign of deep adoration for the imposing Namah Parvat. The lads were moved to imitate Mauktik's behaviour by the significance of his deeds, which struck them like a resonating chord. They did an act of adoration alongside Mauktik as a result of a deep wellspring of affection that erupted inside them. The view of Namah Parvat assumed an even more extraordinary visage, enhanced by the presence of a golden cloud that adorned the background, reminiscent of a hair bun, and the moon, partially covered by another cloud, appearing as a crescent, emerged shyly from its celestial abode.

They remained fixed in this sacred moment, a picture of astonishment and reverence. For several minutes, they were surrounded by silence, which intertwined with the breathtaking scenery before them. It was a frozen moment, an experience that would live on in their recollections as the crowning treasure of a lifetime.

Following an extended period of silence, Arjun remarked, "It's as if everyone has been rendered speechless, as if we're all high on something."

In response, Mauktik offered a natural explanation: "Indeed, the Himalay have that effect. Such an environment is induced by high altitude."

The group's laughter punctuated the tranquil environment, creating a ripple of amusement. Mauktik's response remained enigmatic, unable to fathom the source of their amusement at his innocence.

Arjun, on the other hand, attempted to express his awe in words, expressing the sensation that they all shared. "It is truly beyond words. I've never felt such deep contentment from witnessing something before."

Akash quickly agreed, his answer echoing, "Absolutely."

Aditya added his voice to the chorus of agreement, saying, "Absolutely right."

"So, where do we proceed from here?" Arjun inquired.

"And where's our little guide?" Akash said, his brow furrowed in search of their four-legged acquaintance. "I appear to have lost track of it."

Aditya, who was equally perplexed, asked, “Yeah, where’s the dog gone?”

Arjun’s words were filled with self-pity; a sardonic smirk accompanied his statement, “Losing a brown dog against this expansive white canvas of snow is truly a pathetic feat.”

Though they searched for a response, Mauktik remained mute, his gaze exploring the surroundings in search of the missing dog. An unexpected tremor rippled through the ground beneath them, jolting them awake from their stupor.

“I’m starting to feel a little lightheaded, guys,” Arjun said, his voice concerned.

Akash’s voice became urgent in response to his observation, carrying over the wind: “Hold tight, everyone! It’s an earthquake. Keep your wits about you.”

Arjun’s remark was tinged with surprise: “Oh!”

The ground beneath their feet trembled for around 9 seconds before gradually subsiding. Mauktik’s acute senses recognised something strange in the middle of this unsettling incident. He offered a fast instruction in his deep and resonant tone, a sense of urgency emphasising his words, “We must move swiftly from this spot. Take a look over there.” His motion drew their attention to the peak looming behind them.

Arjun’s answer was fast and to the point, filled with scepticism: “Seriously? Is there going to be an avalanche now?”

"We need to run, guys!" Aditya's voice screamed, piercing through the air, "We need to run!"

"This way, quickly!" said Mauktik, speaking in a hurried rhythm. "There looks to be a trail running across the slopes."

They pushed themselves forward across the snow-covered ground with a new rush of energy. They were lucky since the freshly fallen snow was just ankle-deep, protecting them from becoming entangled as they ran. The rhythm of their footfall and the whoosh of the wind accentuated their rapid pace. Mauktik was on guard during this anxious rush for safety, following behind to make sure that none of them were caught in the snow's grasp.

The oncoming avalanche approached them with frightening speed. Mauktik's acute eyesight saw a little cave nestled in the far slopes of the mountains while they were sprinting. He understood, however, that the boys would be unable to reach there in time, being entrapped within the snow's grip. Mauktik launched a series of lightning-fast movements, leveraging his exceptional speed. He dragged each youngster to safety one by one, carrying them to the cave before returning to get the next. They were all comfortably ensconced within the sheltering hollow in three quick cycles. The environment around them was consumed almost instantly by the inexorable approach of the avalanche. The area was once again shrouded in dense fog, blocking all visibility.

The guys were taken aback when they discovered Mauktik's action had ensured their lives without their knowledge.

"Your abilities are truly remarkable," Aditya said to Mauktik, "but I must admit, they're somewhat unsettling."

Arjun added a humorous note, his comments tinged with irony: "Yeah, maybe next time you decide to enact such a grand rescue, just drop us a hint in advance so we can mentally prepare ourselves."

"I apologise sincerely, but I was left with no choice," Mauktik said meekly, bending and joining his hands together. "My quick action was critical; otherwise, you might have been buried beneath the snow." The weight of his comments hung heavy on the assembly, producing contemplative quiet.

"Have either of you noticed how Mauktik incorporates numerous gestures from our culture?" Arjun asked Akash and Aditya softly.

Akash acknowledged quietly, "Indeed, he greets and apologises with the traditional gesture of joining hands."

"And remember how he knelt and offered prayers to Namah Parvat?" Aditya added as his voice dropped.

"Should we ask him about his familiarity with these customs?" Akash wondered, his voice quiet.

"I doubt it will yield much," Aditya responded with pessimism. "He'll most likely respond in enigmatic fashion, 'I cannot say anything,' hence there's no point."

"That's a good point," Arjun said ironically, gesticulating towards Aditya.

Mauktik's voice rang out from behind them, taking them off guard. "Excuse me! I apologise for intruding, but I can hear your whispers. So there's no reason to keep your voices down." Once again, the boys were taken aback by his revelation.

Peace was gradually restored. The avalanche's relentless onslaught had paused, and as the sun fell below the horizon, darkness descended on the area. The boys were seated within the cave's shelter, fighting with the falling temperature, their shivering testimony to the decreasing atmosphere. Meanwhile, Mauktik positioned himself at the cave's entrance, their tranquil pose framed by the snow-covered surroundings.

Among the silence, Akash asked, "Are we considering spending the night here?"

"I'm not sure," Aditya said, his voice trembling. "It appears safe, but I'm still concerned about what happened to the dog. I can only hope it's not injured and isn't stuck in the snow."

Arjun's restlessness inside the cave led him to a discovery that disturbed the silence with a quick exclamation, "Hey, guys, come over here! There's something interesting here."

The intensity of his tone drew Akash and Aditya to his side. Their attention was drawn to a narrow and hidden underground entrance. "Do you think we can explore this?" Arjun's remark hung in the air, overflowing with excitement.

"Are you out of your mind?" Akash said, his voice tinted with scepticism. "You want to go into the depths of a mountain now? There was an earthquake just an hour ago."

"Indeed, Arjun," Aditya agreed, a tinge of caution in his voice. "It's a risky proposition."

Nonetheless, Arjun's logic emerged, grounded in his thirst: "But I'm quite parched. I was hoping to find a source of underground water."

Mauktik, ever vigilant, inspected the passage from their vantage point, providing soothing words: "Allow me to investigate on your behalf."

Arjun examined the passage with a critical eye, concluding, "I doubt any of us could pass through that space; it's far too confined."

"Don't worry about that," Mauktik suggested. "All three of you need to do is take a step back from the passage." What happened next took the boys by surprise yet again, causing them to question their assumptions yet further.

Mauktik dashed for the passage with unfathomable speed, disappearing into thin air as a faint shockwave trailed behind, aglow with a vibrant cerulean colour. Befuddlement hung in the air, epitomised by Aditya's question, "What just happened? Where is he?"

"Mauktik, where are you?" exclaimed Arjun with concern.

"Guys, I am inside now," a resonant, gravelly voice issued from the depths of the passage a few heartbeats later. "You should come in; this place is amazing."

Aditya's response was astonished: "He's inside now? Can he genuinely do this?"

Akash wondered, "I am utterly amazed by him."

Arjun said, echoing their amazement. "I wish I had his abilities."

After a short while, there was a rumbling from below, and Mauktik's voice could be heard calling out, "You can enter now; I've cleared the way." Without saying a word, the boys entered one by one.

"It's extremely dark in here," Akash noted in the pitch blackness. "Nothing can be seen by us."

Their predicament was confirmed by Aditya, who said, "The batteries in our torches and headlamps have also depleted."

A sudden flash of light illuminated the area and identified Mauktik as its source. His closed fists glowed brilliantly with blue light. They began heading into the narrow tunnel, surrounded by rocky limitations on all sides, with cautious steps.

Arjun started the conversation by asking, "Mauktik, may I pose a question to you?" His curiosity peaked.

Mauktik nodded in response to the question, saying, "Certainly, feel free."

"How did you appear here after disappearing into thin air?" Arjun questioned.

"Ah, that is one of my unique abilities, what we refer to as *Antarhita*," Mauktik explained.

Aditya inquired further, "What does that mean?" Mauktik provided a straightforward translation: "In your language, it's teleportation."

After seeing a linguistic similarity, Arjun continued, "Your language has a striking resemblance to Sanskrit. How did you learn about it?"

Mauktik recognised the connection by saying, "Yes, we, among our race, employ Sanskrit. You must be curious to learn how we came to speak your language and how we communicate with one another. I must stress again that I am unable to provide this information."

When asked again, "Why do your hands emit a blue glow?" Arjun persisted.

"The science behind it is quite intricate, but put simply, it's due to the presence of nitrogen in our bodies," Mauktik said to begin a brief explanation. "We breathe in nitrogen from the atmosphere."

Akash marvelled, "Remarkable. Aliens can be so distinct yet astonishing."

As they continued their journey, the tunnel gradually expanded. Their eyes darted around, searching for a water source, but they were met only with solid rock. Eventually, they reached a spacious chamber reminiscent of the sheltered cave they had encountered on the opposite side.

The chamber they entered felt warmer compared to the tunnel they had traversed. Fortunately, they noticed water streaming down in a conical shape from one of the upper walls. At the base, a puddle was created by the trickling water. "Look," said Arjun, "I think we can drink this water."

Aditya agreed and said, "Yes, I think so. It ought to be fresh water."

They shaped their hands into cups and drank from the puddle to alleviate their thirst. After the lads had finished their drinks, Mauktik came over to join them, but not before he took a sip and gave the water a little touch to his forehead in respect.

This time, Aditya's curiosity got the better of him, and he said, "We've noticed that your gestures closely mimic those from our ancient customs. We're truly curious about how you become aware of everything." Mauktik didn't say anything. They all sat in contemplative silence for a while, recognising that there was no apparent exit and that it appeared to be a dead end.

After a while, Mauktik said, "I sense a draft of cold air inside; it appears to be coming from somewhere nearby." Mauktik painstakingly looked in every crevice of the cave but found nothing. Then a thought occurred to Mauktik, and it pointed its clenched fist upward. The ceiling of the cave was covered with thick, white ice. Mauktik saw a little gap in the ceiling that could only accommodate one person at a time.

Turning towards the guys, Mauktik stated, "Stay here; I'll look outside."

Mauktik rose and slipped through the opening with a beautiful leap.

The youngsters thought about their predicament after being left in the cave alone. "Have you ever considered how peculiarly we're moving towards Mauktik's destination instead of ours?" asked Arjun, expressing his ideas.

"Yeah, I totally forgot about that," Akash added.

"For the time being, we have no choice but to follow his lead," Aditya continued. "We need to escape this situation because we are trapped here. He appears to be the only one who can assist us. In addition, the dog, not Mauktik, guided us here before. I think he's really trying to help us."

When Mauktik went outside to look around, it found a large area of snow-covered ground that rapidly transformed into a rocky environment. The once-overcast weather had cleared, and the entire scene was illuminated by the full moon's gentle brightness.

When Mauktik entered the cave again, he announced, "The weather has cleared outside, and I've found a nice area where you may set up your campground. Although it's quite a journey, I think it's the best choice."

Curious, Aditya inquired, "Why can't we stay here and set up camp? It seems completely enclosed and secure from all sides. I can't imagine a safer spot."

"You might be overlooking the fact that we're likely at the base of a mountain, and there was an earthquake just a few hours ago," Mauktik said carefully. "There may still be aftershocks; therefore, we should probably leave this place as soon as possible."

Arjun agreed, saying, "That does make sense."

Akash concurred, saying, "I'm on board with that."

"Let's exit one by one," Mauktik advised. Mauktik lifted and transported each of them through the narrow opening with remarkable quickness, softly placing them outside. The beautiful vista awed the youngsters once everyone was assembled. The snow-covered countryside, bathed in moonlight, exuded a weird and peaceful vibe.

"So, which way do we need to go?" Aditya spoke softly.

"Over there," Mauktik said, pointing northward, "it appears to be a small forested area beyond the rocky terrain, approximately 2 kilometres from here."

They began their journey across the undulating ground under the moonlight. The boys had an easy time descending because it was gradual. Aditya struck up a discussion as they moved from icy trails to solid rocky ground, saying, "You know, we've been on the move the entire day, but I don't feel tired at all."

“I completely agree,” Arjun said. “I’m feeling remarkably revitalised. It’s almost as if the mountain air had a renewing impact.”

Akash expressed his views: “You know what just crossed my mind? Sharad.”

“Yeah, I can only imagine how worried he must be looking for us,” Aditya said, nodding.

Meanwhile, on the flip side, Sharad and the rescue team had laboriously searched the area all day long, but despite their efforts, they had not found any information concerning the boys’ whereabouts. They returned to the campground that Sharad had originally set up, as it had grown dark where they were as well.

“We’ll resume looking for the boys tomorrow,” the group’s leader said in a solemn voice. “I’ve enlisted more folks to assist us. If we can’t find them by tomorrow, we might have to break the bad news to their families that they are likely dead.” This announcement caught everyone’s attention, and Sharad’s expression grew gloomy. He grappled with the sinking feeling that the boys might not have survived this ordeal, a situation he had never before encountered in all his years of leading treks. This gave him a sickening sense. His spirit had been severely wounded by this tragedy.

Returning to the other side, the boys and Mauktik continued their journey. “How much further do we have to travel, Mauktik?” asked Akash.

Mauktik answered, "I think we're getting there. Soon the forest will start to appear, and soon after we enter it, we'll set up camp."

Another query from Aditya was, "Mauktik, what's your plan from here?"

"My destination is to meet Brahmarishi," Mauktik retorted, "and that remains unchanged."

"But we don't know who Brahmarishi is or where he lives, and we might not even be going in his direction," Aditya continued. "So why do you continue to travel with us?"

Mauktik said quietly, "I cannot say for certain about all of you, but I have a strong sense that you will lead me to him." The youngsters were perplexed by Mauktik's reply.

"Do you have any information about the place where you intend to find Brahmarishi?" Arjun inquired in an effort to gain more clarification.

"No, I've never been there before," Mauktik retorted. "It's an ashram in the Himalay somewhere."

They soon arrived at the beginning of the forest, and as they went farther in, the area grew darker due to the presence of tall, dense trees. The lads found it difficult to see, but Mauktik's improved vision made it simple for them. Once more forming luminous fists, Mauktik illuminated the boys' way and provided them with directional assistance. They eventually found a good place to camp.

Before starting to set up camp, the boys lowered their luggage to the ground and took a short break. "Why don't you go with Mauktik and gather some logs for the campfire?" Aditya offered Akash. "Arjun and I will set up the camp in the interim."

Arjun added, "That sounds like a good idea, but while Mauktik is away, we'll need a source of light to pitch the tent."

"Akash, didn't you have a lighter?" Aditya recalled. "While we wait for you to return with additional firewood, we can use it to light one of the logs and manage our tasks."

Akash sadly acknowledged, "I believe I lost the lighter. When we were in the cave, I looked for it but was unable to locate it."

"Don't worry; I can help with that," said Mauktik as it offered its support. It quickly gathered a number of branches and dried twigs from the vicinity, forming a pile. Mauktik produced a flash of blue flame at the tip of the branch it was holding in its grasp, lighting the pile on fire. "There you go," Mauktik said.

Everyone was in wonder as the branches now blazed with the customary yellow and crimson flames. Akash said, "Wow, that was incredible."

Arjun closely watched the flames created by an energy flow through Mauktik's hand, which was channelled from the base to the tip of the branch he held. "May I hold that branch?" he inquired. "No, it's hot and won't burn if I release it," Mauktik retorted.

"You're a very remarkable being," Arjun praised. "We wished we had such talents."

"Thank you," Mauktik retorted. "You three may stay here and erect the tent while I gather more branches."

The lads all uttered the same word of gratitude: "Thanks."

Mauktik lit its fist once more and went into the forest, leaving the guys to finish setting up the tent. At this point, Aditya asked, "Do you guys feel anything odd? I no longer feel as cold."

Akash added, "I was just thinking the same thing."

"I'm still wondering if all of this is true," Arjun pondered aloud. "Is it feasible that I'm in a dream or, worse, an alternate reality?"

The sentiment was mirrored by Aditya, who said, "Everything feels really weird. We got lost, ran into an alien who saved us, and are now travelling to an unidentified location."

Akash stepped in and said, "I just remembered..."

"Your lighter?" Arjun retorted immediately.

"No, not that," Akash clarified. "I distinctly recall warming up after drinking that mountain-sourced water."

"You're correct; it was a small quantity, but now I feel strangely at ease with the cold," Aditya recalled.

Arjun pondered, “I can’t help but wonder about the mysteries concealed within these colossal mountains.”

After returning with a bundle of branches, Mauktik scattered some of them on the pile of burning materials. The boys had completed setting up the tent in the meantime. “Mauktik, don’t add any more wood to the fire; we’ll shortly be entering the tent,” said Aditya.

Mauktik gave his approval by saying, “Okay.”

“Do we have any food?” asked Akash.

“Are you feeling hungry?” Aditya asked him as he turned the question back to him.

Akash answered, “Well, not exactly, just curious.”

“Well, you probably are hungry,” Aditya said. “Despite the fact that we haven’t eaten since the afternoon, I don’t feel particularly peckish.”

Akash nodded in agreement and said, “Yeah, me neither.”

Then Arjun said, “Perhaps that water filled our stomachs as well.” They all shared a laugh, and Mauktik added, “I think there was something special in the water; I feel incredibly energised.”

“There you go,” Arjun remarked.

They continued talking before deciding to take a nap. Mauktik jumped onto a branch of a tall tree and made himself comfortable for the night as the boys withdrew inside the tent.

The boys were all nestled inside their tent and were just about to nod off when they heard something. It seemed to be coming from a great distance. "Do you hear that?" Akash whispered as he slept next to Arjun.

Arjun answered, "Yes."

They were forced to sit up as the noise grew louder, straining their ears to make out what it was. As the sound became clearer, they found it challenging to determine its nature. Aditya inquired, sounding concerned, "What's that?" Arjun and Akash exchanged perplexed looks, indicating that they were unsure of the origin of the noise.

When the bonfire outside had diminished and was only providing a weak orange glow, they made the decision to exit the tent.

Akash sounded cautious and yelled, "Mauktik? Are you close by?"

In response, Mauktik gently stepped down from the tree branch and acknowledged its existence with a straightforward "Yes."

Still curious, Akash questioned, "Did you hear that too?"

The eerie sound reverberated throughout the woodland. Mauktik acknowledged that it had heard it by nodding.

"Could it be a ghost or something else?" Aditya wondered with curiosity and a hint of dread. "Who would be out and about in the middle of the night like this?"

"It's quite unlikely to be a ghost," Mauktik told them after shining some light on the scenario. "A shaankh is being blown, which is frequently used to drive away evil spirits."

"You seem more familiar with our culture than we are," Akash remarked in awe.

The eerie sound stopped, and they saw a yellowish-orange light coming their way. Unsure of whether the source of the sound constituted a threat or provided assistance, Mauktik refrained from illuminating its hands, preferring to remain undetectable. "There is something out there," Arjun remarked. "A light is getting closer."

They were given unshakeable assurance by Mauktik, who said, "Don't worry; I'm here with you."

Arjun continued jokingly, "In fact, without you, I might have fainted already," as he took comfort in Mauktik's company. All of them stared intently at the growing light, their curiosity reaching its zenith.

Chapter 7:

A Place Beyond the 3 Dimensions

As the soft, yellowish-orange glow expanded, it gradually revealed a human silhouette holding the light. It was clear that this person was aware of their presence and was steadily approaching. In response, Mauktik decided to illuminate his hands to better discern the approaching figure, who was now quite close.

The identity of the approaching person was ultimately revealed when their surroundings were illuminated by this fresh illumination. This enigmatic figure was an elderly man wearing saffron robes and holding a shaankh in his right hand and a lantern in his left. With long, matted hair tangled into complicated strands and a flowing, silver beard spilling down to his chest, his appearance spoke of age. Although he had wrinkles on his face, they didn't hide the youthful vigour in his eyes. The man steadily drew closer to them while walking barefoot.

Akash questioned, "Is it common to encounter a Saadhu Baba in these mountains, especially at such late hours?"

"Sincerely, buddy, I have no idea," Aditya said. "I'm already bewildered."

He appeared to be in his seventies or eighties as the Saadhu approached them and stood in front of the group. The Saadhu's eyes locked into Mauktik's with a calm look and a flimsy smile before remaining on each of their faces for a prolonged period of time. It was interesting to see that this visitor didn't act surprised or curious when he first saw Mauktik, despite the fact that the creature's hands were glowing blue.

The Saadhu said, "Brahmarishi has been waiting for you," in a voice that resounded with profound serenity and comforting wisdom.

In the next moment, Mauktik's radiant hands dimmed, and with a humble gesture, he lowered his head and clasped his hands together, offering a reverent "Pranam." The boys, sensing the solemnity of the situation, emulated Mauktik's gesture in respectful unison. The Saadhu, reciprocating their gesture of respect, replied with a benevolent blessing, "Ayushman Bhava."

He then gestured for them to follow him, prompting Mauktik to express concern in an urgent tone: "But, baba, should they come with us? I was aware that only those summoned or invited were permitted to enter."

"Yes, you are correct," the Saadhu said in response to Mauktik's observation. "Only those who have been invited are permitted to enter."

Mauktik fell silent as a result of this response. His face was hidden by his shroud, making the boys unable to read his emotions or fathom his intentions. As a result, the boys found themselves perplexed.

In an attempt to solve the mystery surrounding their circumstance, Akash asked, "What's going on? Where are we going?"

The Saadhu's response was enigmatic, leaving them with more questions than answers, only assuring them, "You will see soon enough."

Arjun kindly asked, "Can you please take us to a place from where we can make our way back home?" as he felt an overwhelming pull to return home.

Aditya, on the other hand, had a different viewpoint and was anxious to learn more about the magical voyage. "All these extraordinary experiences we've had—it's been truly magical," he said, expressing his feelings. "I'm interested to see what else lies ahead."

This view was shared by Akash, who said, "I don't mind spending a little longer in a world beyond the ordinary."

Arjun eventually gave in and agreed to join them on their unexpected excursion after taking into account the bonds of friendship. "Okay, I'll go with you guys, but we have to get back within two days," he said. "Our loved ones will undoubtedly have been worried about us."

The Saadhu didn't say a word until everyone agreed with his idea, at which point he started them on their journey. He moved deeper into the dense jungle while holding his lantern high and creating unsettling shadows among the trees. Following in his footsteps, the boys did so, with Mauktik coming in last. Mauktik soon realised that the boys couldn't adequately navigate the forest trail with the Saadhu's lantern's meagre light. He sent forth the gentle blue radiance from his hands once more as he became aware of their effort, illuminating the path in front of them.

Arjun's hushed talk with Akash and Aditya sporadically shattered the shroud of stillness as they continued on their mystery adventure. "Why did the Saadhu mention that no one ought to visit this place without an invitation?" Arjun inquired quietly about Akash and Aditya as they walked. "It makes me very concerned about their motives."

"No idea, bro," Akash replied, while Arjun admitted, "I just want to make it clear: if this venture takes a dangerous turn, I'd rather not be a part of it."

Aditya, on the other hand, exhibited a curious yet cautious expression. "We'll monitor our route and then return; I'm most interested in Mauktik's mission and all the mystery surrounding it," he said.

Arjun silently signalled his agreement with Aditya, giving them a thumbs-up.

"Guys, I know you're whispering, but both the Saadhu Baba and I can hear you well," Mauktik said as he went closer to the guys. Mauktik was constantly on the lookout for their remarks. "Whispering is useless in this situation."

The boys became silent once more as they continued their journey into the jungle, flanked by the Saadhu and Mauktik, their goal and fate still unknown. They emerged into a moonlit clearing after an hour and a half of drifting through the jungle. The moon's ethereal radiance and the shimmering stars provided a peaceful backdrop. The grass in this open area was noticeably shorter than in the surrounding forest, and it was scattered with little, untamed plants and vibrant flowers.

Arjun, ever the astute observer, couldn't help but comment on this unexpected revelation. "So, it appears that people here like gardening!" he said. Following his exclamation, the guys were shocked by Mauktik's gentle, quick burst of giggling. They swivelled their heads to see if Mauktik was the cause of the strange noise, and he was a little embarrassed by his own actions.

Meanwhile, the Saadhu, who had been peacefully studying a massive tree, turned abruptly towards them and said, "Wait here and rest. I'll be back shortly." With those remarks, he vanished behind the big tree trunk, leaving the youngsters wondering what would happen next.

On the soft grass, they gathered together, creating a square, and faced each other. Mauktik was now more comfortable sitting among the boys, although he still had some doubts. He was puzzled as to why they, too, were a part of this enigmatic gathering due to a lingering interest, though. As they settled in, a curious exchange of glances unfolded between the boys and Mauktik, who sat among them with his eyes radiating their signature sparkling blue.

This period of silence was broken by Akash's query, "Now what?"

Aditya struggled to respond and said, "No idea."

Mauktik, who appeared to be equally perplexed, was compelled to ask for an explanation. He asked, "Did any of you have any inkling that you were called or invited here?"

Akash shook his head emphatically. "Not at all. We actually thought you brought us here," he replied.

Mauktik clarified, "I brought you all into this forest solely for the purpose of setting up camp," in an effort to make clear his role in the current occurrences.

Arjun said, observing the peculiar character of their surroundings and his propensity towards abnormalities. He thought, "This forest is extremely odd."

"Indeed," replied Aditya, who appeared to be equally as astonished by the startling change from the rocky terrain to the forest. "Usually, forests don't start up straight after such a rough area."

Ever the pragmatist, Akash saw a connection between their predicament now and their journey through the mountain's cave. "Since we entered that tunnel inside the mountain," he added, "it seems that everything has taken on an air of mysticism."

Arjun asked Mauktik about the prophecy and their part in his mission before turning back to them. "So, according to your prophecy, our part in your journey wasn't specified?"

With clarity, Mauktik answered, "No, the prophecy only revealed that you would lead me here and nothing more." The boys and Mauktik were equally perplexed by the mysterious nature of their involvement in this developing story, and their interest grew with each passing second.

The Saadhu reappeared in their midst in a short span. They all rose to their feet with zeal. The Saadhu took a seat in front of the massive tree trunk, clasping his hands, sitting in a padmasan posture, and closing his eyes as he began to recite something. To the boys' surprise, a faint glimmer appeared at the centre of the tree trunk, gradually expanding and intensifying in luminosity. It grew until it was the size of a door, with an elegantly arched upper portion. The boys, on the other hand, could only see a bright white light; nothing lay beyond its glowing threshold. This light's brilliance pleasantly lit their immediate surroundings.

The Saadhu broke the hush by saying, "Now, all of you may enter." Arjun inquired, "So, do we go through the tree?" The Saadhu confirmed his statement with a pleasant smile in return.

They were abruptly stopped by Mauktik, who reminded them to take off their shoes before continuing. The boys removed their shoes as a result, and Mauktik added, "You may leave them behind the tree," while subtly eyeing the Saadhu for approval. The Saadhu kept his soft smile on. The boys then each made their way through the enchanted passageway in the tree, followed by Mauktik and the Saadhu. As they moved, the brilliant light gradually grew smaller until it finally disappeared, leaving the tranquil atmosphere of the forest unaltered.

The brilliant light forced the boys to avert their eyes as they ventured deeper into the tree. Mauktik and the Saadhu, on the other hand, didn't seem to be bothered by the light. The guys began to feel a difference in the ground under them gradually after some time. It felt like they were walking on fresh, pliable grass, and their surroundings had a pleasant, ambient aroma. Their senses were awakened by the wonderful aroma that surrounded them. Encouraged, the guys made the decision to open their eyes, letting their vision slowly adjust to this unfamiliar scene. What caught their attention resembled something straight out of a fairy tale. A flawless, cerulean sky with sporadic clouds that were bathed in the sun's warmth stretched over them.

In every direction, their eyes were met with a sea of emerald plants and trees that stretched as far as the eye could see. Almost all of the plants produced bright flowers, and the vibrant hues of their blooms painted the landscape. Unfamiliar fruits dangling from some trees piqued their interest. They came upon trees and plants among the foliage that they had never seen before, giving the setting an aura of enchantment. With rough terrain to their left, the gorgeous snow-capped mountains in the southern distance added depth to the landscape's variety. The presence of colourful birds and butterflies, whose beautiful flight accentuated the attractiveness of this magical area, further exposed the surroundings.

Even Mauktik was entranced by the breathtaking surroundings, marvelling. Arjun nervously questioned, "Are we in heaven?" as he was overcome by the place's extreme perfection. The group didn't respond to the question, choosing instead to savour the ethereal beauty that surrounded them. Everything about it projected a spotless, never-ending magnificence, as though it had been lovingly maintained by hands we could not see.

The Saadhu motioned for them to follow once more, and they obediently followed, beginning this amazing adventure across the paradisiacal scenery.

They continued their stroll on grass that was as deliciously smooth underfoot as a carpet. They saw many people along the way who were all dressed in holy attire and had the manners of saints and monks. Notably, these people came not just from India but also from many parts of the world, as seen by the diversity of their appearances. They passed by modest homes with thatched roofs made of a combination of wood, stone, and mud as they travelled. No inquiries were asked despite the intense curiosity that surrounded them as they silently followed the Saadhu towards an unknown destination.

They sauntered down the banks of a large lake, where their course had taken them. The lake was given a golden colour by the sun's brilliant reflection, a stunning sight to behold. Their enchanted journey went on with each step. After about 20 minutes, they arrived at the banks of a small river. From the mountain peaks that gave birth to this river, a spectacular waterfall cascaded elegantly into the distance. A raised area studded with massive boulders was hidden along the riverbank. But they couldn't help but focus on a saint who was serenely perched on one of the boulders and was dressed in immaculate white clothing. Under the shady embrace of a gigantic banyan tree with a huge trunk, the saint was totally absorbed in meditation.

The saint, who appeared to be in his sixties, had flowing, unbound silver hair and a beard that was also silver in colour. His face, absorbed in meditation, radiated an unruffled tranquillity. They immediately became aware that the Saadhu had stopped as they stood in silent adoration. They turned to look at him, and he gestured towards the meditating saint. Mauktik knew instinctively that they were where they were supposed to be. The Saadhu left, taking a different route.

The boys and Mauktik stood calmly before the saint, respecting his state of meditation as they carefully observed their surroundings. The duration of their vigil was brief since Brahmarishi immediately opened his eyes. He had a profound presence and a fascinating, brilliant stare that gave off an undeniable impression of holiness. Brahmarishi moved his focus to the quartet while wearing a soft smile on his face.

"Pranam Brahmarishi," Mauktik said as he walked up to the saint, his voice now taking on a feminine tone. She then joined her hands in greeting and made a small bow. Mauktik gradually revealed her face after removing her hood and face mask for the first time since meeting the boys, doing so with an attitude of reverence. She bowed down before the saint and delicately touched the same rock with her forehead that Brahmarishi had been contemplating.

Brahmarishi responded by saying "Swagatam" and extended his right hand, palm outstretched, and giving her a comforting, kind blessing.

Arjun, who couldn't contain his amazement, exclaimed in a loud voice, "Mauktik is a girl!" while the boys took this information in.

Chapter 8:

The Stranger's Identity

The boys were left in a state of complete disbelief and profound astonishment upon discovering Mauktik's true identity. Now, before them stood a tall, robust young woman-like figure with a mane of dense, silvery hair cascading down her back, reaching past her waist. In response to Arjun's exclamation, she turned towards the boys, revealing her face to them for the very first time.

They witnessed something that was nothing short of enchanting. Her outstanding attractiveness was enhanced by her big, alluring blue eyes, her well-defined nose, and her delicately pointed chin. Her skin tone was light, almost porcelain-like, with a subtle pinkish-blue undertone that gave off a bright, smooth aspect. Two glistening silver strands that were gently trailing behind her ears, which resembled human ears but had a distinct pointed tip at the top, framed her face. Her general appearance was strikingly similar to that of a human, with one noteworthy exception: three conspicuous, gently arched incisions decorated each side of her neck at a precise angle, an entirely natural feature. As the three boys continued to stare at her in awe, it became clear why Mauktik had kept her true identity hidden; her innate charm could easily attract unwanted attention.

Mauktik turned to face Brahmarishi once more, her words tinted with love and excitement. She introduced herself saying, "I've patiently waited for so many years to finally meet you. My name is Mauktik, and I am Avan's great-great granddaughter."

"Yes, my child, I am well aware of your lineage, and I am delighted that you have found your way here," Brahmarishi said in his calm and deeply resonant heavenly voice.

Mauktik couldn't hold back her excitement as she added, "Avan shared everything about you with me, and based on his descriptions, I recognised you right away." Brahmarishi listened with a soft smile on his face.

The enthusiasm in Mauktik's voice could be felt as she continued, "I assume you are aware of the reason for my coming here. The prophecy stated that I would be able to access the power necessary to protect Nairmanika once I arrived here because it could only be obtained from earth."

Brahmarishi responded wisely, "Indeed, I am aware. You'll get everything you want. It would be best for you all to relax for the time being. You've travelled a tough and protracted route. Spend some time looking around and enjoying this site. We also have some young guests here, and I'm excited to meet them." They then both turned to look at the boys at the same time.

The guys were standing there, their thoughts racing with inquiries, and their eagerness to learn was obvious. Mauktik looked towards Brahmarishi as they arrived and said, "Brahmarishi, I'm still puzzled as to why they are here. I thought this place was off-limits to the general public unless they were invited expressly. They don't know anything about this location and don't seem to be present for any particular reason. I thought that all they had to do was lead me here."

"In this world, everyone has a purpose and a unique role to play in the journey of life, and so do they," Brahmarishi retorted with his trademark serenity. "You'll eventually comprehend their motivation as well."

The youngsters' looks spoke volumes as they moved nearer to the guys. It seemed as though they were seeing Mauktik in a completely new light, one that was very different from the friend they had travelled with up to that point.

In his address to the boys, Brahmarishi recognised their obvious interest in their surroundings. "I can see that you are filled with questions about everything you are witnessing here," he reassured them. "You will, be assured, get responses to all of your questions. But for now, I advise that you all get some much-needed rest and eat something."

Arjun nervously said, "Thank you, but there's one small thing I'd like to inquire about," unable to control his curiosity. With patience, Brahmarishi said, "Of course, my child."

Then Arjun asked, "Am I possibly dead, or is this reality?"

"You are definitely not dead," Brahmarishi responded, breaking into a gentle smile.

Arjun then took a risk and inquired, "So, what is this place? Is there a name for it?"

"In fact, this place has been known by a number of names throughout numerous eras," according to Brahmarishi. "You may refer to it as Jnañā-sthan."

Aditya was ready to ask his queries when Mauktik cut him off by saying, "Alright, everyone, we'll look at all your questions, like Brahmarishi mentioned. But for the time being, let's heed his advice and get some sustenance and rest. You all deserve a break because you've been on such a long journey." As soon as Brahmarishi left, a woman in her forties wearing a white saree made of natural fibres walked over to them.

Her dedication to simplicity and purity was represented by the delicate handwoven designs that decorated the saree. She was wrapped from the shoulders to the ankles in a traditional drape, with the pallu elegantly veiling her head. Her face radiated ageless beauty that was accentuated by a natural glow fostered by this place's peaceful way of life. Her eyes, deep and soulful, sparkled with wisdom. In her gentle, melodious voice, she warmly greeted them, saying, "You are all welcome here. My name is Nishka. Please accompany me." In response, they greeted her with folded hands and a respectful pranam.

Mauktik and the boys followed Nishka as she led them to a nearby cottage. The guys had a tonne of questions concerning the strange events they had seen along the walk, but they showed restraint since they knew the answers would arrive eventually.

Nishka was gracious enough to tell them to wash their hands and feet and sit on the veranda before going inside the cottage. The sadhvi reappeared shortly after they got back, carrying a basket full of fruit that she presented elegantly on banana leaves. The lads were intrigued by Mauktik's quick prayer before her meal because it was the first time they had seen her eat; therefore, it aroused their interest.

Everyone enjoyed their food in silence. After everyone was done, Nishka said, "Allow me to escort you to your cottages, where you can find some rest."

"Will everyone of us have a cottage of our own?" asked Akash.

"No, one for Mauktik and one for the three of you," Nishka answered coolly. Akash acknowledged it with a nod.

The huts had thatched roofs and were all made of mud, stones, and wood. Before departing, Nishka led them to their individual lodgings. The boys and Mauktik entered their designated dwellings after a short excursion.

They entered and placed their belongings in a corner of the space. All three of them decided to take a quick nap, as they were all feeling very tired. They had little energy for conversation due to their tiredness.

Aditya woke up about 3 hours later to discover Arjun and Akash gone from the room. He went outside and saw his two friends enjoying the peaceful sunset while they were settled on the veranda. Mauktik wandered aimlessly nearby. Aditya joined the boys, and while they took in the splendour of the sunset, Mauktik noticed their alertness and walked over to them.

"I hope you rested well," she inquired.

With the words "Yes, thanks, but how about you?" Akash gave her assurance.

"I took a little time to rest," Mauktik retorted. "All of you are awake now, so let's visit Brahmarishi."

The guys got on their feet, and they all made their way back to where they had first seen Brahmarishi. They discovered him there and engaged in a discussion with other saints, who left right away as soon as they got there. "Pranam Brahmarishi, is this a suitable time for discussion?" Mauktik asked him.

He then said, "Yes, my child, please feel free to ask any questions that have been weighing on your mind."

"You explained that they are involved in my search," Mauktik inquired. "I'm interested in learning more about that."

Brahmarishi agreed, "Certainly. However, before we delve into that, I would like you to share with them information about yourself, your quest, and Ganagrah."

Aditya interjected, "But she previously mentioned that she couldn't disclose details about herself or her quest."

Mauktik clarified, "That's correct, but if Brahmarishi is requesting this, there must be a reason why you all should know about me."

Arjun voiced his worries about going back home, but Mauktik gave him a severe look for it. While Arjun was worried about leaving, Akash and Aditya were eager to learn more about Mauktik and her people.

After pausing to think in silence for a minute, Mauktik mumbled to herself, "Hmm... where should I begin?"

In response, Brahmarishi said, "Why not begin from Janatig's beginning?"

Mauktik agreed, saying, "Yes, I can give them a thorough start."

With a pleasant smile, Brahmarishi continued, "Perhaps you could even show them." When Mauktik saw what he was getting at, she joined her hands and said, "Evam."

Chapter 9:

Ganagrah

The serene atmosphere of the location grew darker as the sun fell below the horizon. Each hut's hallway was lined with illuminated diyas, which produced a cosy, flickering glow. The mysterious ambience was enhanced by some of these diyas that were also affixed to the bases of some Tulsi plants nearby. Mauktik gracefully got into the padmasan position and began to chant something in low tones as she prepared to tell her story and the essence of her kind. Gradually, she fell silent, and a brilliant beam shot from her forehead, forming a circle of light on the large tree trunk next to Brahmarishi. Once more, Mauktik's exceptional skills enthralled the boys. Soon, faint projection-like images began to take shape within the glowing patterns on the tree trunk. Mauktik began her narrative alongside these ethereal visuals.

"Ganagrah, a world in a realm far from earth, is home to living types unrelated to those on your planet. We Janatigs are one of these indigenous species on this planet. While the vegetation on our planet is fairly similar to that on earth, there are several significant differences. Unlike earth, our planet orbits between two twin stars in a binary system, tracing a path similar to the shape of infinity. The enormous distance that separates these 2 stars, which are known as Radnya and Ridham, allows for this cosmic dance. A complete revolution around each star takes a staggering 108 earth years, with each season lasting for thousands of days on end. Remarkably, because of our planet's same size and rotation, our days and nights are similar to those on earth.

When seen from the far reaches of space, our planet appears to be a vibrantly green oasis with immense stretches of water and densely forested land. We, the Janatigs, are the lone humanoid race and the most sophisticated form of life on our planet, which is strange because we lack the diversity of civilisations that earth possesses. We are a small community that inhabits a remote island away from the rest of the world's residents and has a nearly equal distribution of males and females.

We have never participated in trade or business, departing from earth's customs. Here, every individual contributes their skills to various sectors and willingly shares their produce with others. Since the beginning of time, this custom has been an essential component of our culture and has helped to maintain an unwavering feeling of unity among our people. Our founders left us with the following guiding principle: *Life is meaningful only when lived for others*."

"May I inquire about something?" Arjun asked.

Mauktik acknowledged the inquiry with a comforting gesture: "Certainly, go ahead."

"Earlier, you mentioned travelling to our planet via a black hole," Arjun said. "I believe your species has a better comprehension of the cosmos than we do, but how did you know that earth would be your destination when entering a black hole?"

"Well, the initial consideration revolves around the size of the black hole, which should be extremely massive, at least 7 times greater than your solar system," Mauktik said thoughtfully. "As a result, it is dependent on intricate mathematical calculations that take into consideration the coordinates of the cosmic tunnel at a specific time and its specific nature. Another critical factor is determining the tunnel's exit point with regard to time. It's likely that the temporal dimension when entering the cosmic tunnel differs from the temporal dimension when exiting it. Because these tunnels travel across space at extremely high speeds, time is measured in nanoseconds. We can determine not only the world we'll emerge in but also the specific coordinates within that specific universe by measuring its size, rotational patterns, and mass accumulation through accurate computations."

"Wait, are you suggesting that there are multiple universes?" Aditya's curiosity grew.

"Indeed, according to a well-established theory, universes can be imagined as distinct bubbles within the vast expanse of empty space," Mauktik explained further. "These worlds can exist alone or in groups in some situations. What's incredibly intriguing is that we happen to live in one of these clusters, which consists of seven interconnected universe bubbles. Consider varied volumes of soap bubbles to better understand this concept. When two soap bubbles collide, they do not blend completely; rather, they are separated by a thin, filmy wall. Consider the same concept in terms of universes. Each universe bubble contains an entire cosmos within itself. The walls of these universe bubbles are bound by enormously intense gravitational forces. When seven of these universe bubbles combine to form a cluster, they provide a unique spatial structure resembling a pentagonal prism in the centre. This core area, where we are currently, exists in the sixth dimension and serves as a crossroads, facilitating passage between universes inside the cluster. It is theorised that certain entities exist within these seven universes that exhibit either identical or extremely similar traits, following almost identical temporal patterns and events. However, each world has its own unique set of distinctive characteristics. As a result, travelling between these universes is rare and necessitates waiting for the precise conditions to align."

"My mind is utterly blown!" remarked Aditya, plainly in awe.

Akash said, "So, when you mentioned identical or similar objects in these seven universes, were you referring to Earth and Ganagrah?" as a follow-up.

"Yes, exactly," Mauktik replied in agreement. "In two of these universes, Earth and Ganagrah are somewhat like siblings."

"Does this imply that there are planets like ours in other universes?" Akash continued to inquire. "Have any of them been encountered by you?"

Mauktik explained, "While we are aware of another planet in a different universe apart from earth, we still lack substantial information about it."

"We arrived at Jnañā-sthan from earth by crossing the mountains, right?" Arjun was intrigued by the entrances to this location. "Do you have a connection to this location through a comparable gateway on Ganagrah?"

In response, Mauktik said, "Not right now. As far as we are aware, only earth serves as a gateway for travel to Jnañā-sthan. The Himalay mountains were formed long ago to hide it from plain sight, making sure that only those with a true purpose for this area could find their way here."

"What about other universes and planets like our own?" asked Aditya. "Can they enter this location?"

"We don't currently have any information on that front," Mauktik retorted. "It would probably have been discovered if beings from other universes had visited this location in the past. However, as things are, only earth provides access to the portal. However, if we have knowledge of a certain destination, we can travel there from here and to everywhere in the cosmos."

"I see," Aditya said as he nodded in understanding.

Mauktik said, "So, as I was describing, there exists a planet comparable to ours in every universe, sharing some common characteristics and, to some extent, a parallel flow of time and events. You might remember the enormous asteroid that wiped out a large portion of earth's life."

Collectively, the boys nodded in agreement.

"Well, an event of a similar nature took place on our planet," she continued. "Our planet experienced the horrific impact of a large asteroid about 1.5 million earth years ago. Most of the life on our planet was wiped out by this occurrence. Only a small number of organisms were able to survive by hiding in the depths of the oceans, safe from the asteroid's destruction. The atmospheric conditions on our planet were also significantly changed by the asteroid impact. The oxygen content of the atmosphere substantially decreased. Our forefathers, the primitive Janatigs, were among the fortunate survivors. The aquatic life was also contaminated by the asteroid's impact zone. During this turbulent time, a unique occurrence took place when our species was on the verge of extinction."

She continued, "The asteroid itself carried within it a massive purple crystalline structure. It is believed that this crystalline entity was somehow active when the asteroid struck our planet, emanating a certain form of energy that played a pivotal role in assisting our primitive ancestors' survival. The pollution of the oceans forced them to adapt to a terrestrial existence, and this transition led to significant mutations in our cells. Our ability to respire nitrogen due to the scarcity of oxygen was a direct result of these changes. Over countless generations, this transformation shaped us into what we are today," Mauktik said, referring to herself.

Arjun, intrigued, inquired further, "So, the distinctive marks on your neck, are they similar to gills?"

Mauktik replied, "Indeed, these gills allow us to breathe underwater as well."

Akash sought additional information, asking, "And what about this crystalline entity? Does it still exist on your planet?"

Mauktik responded affirmatively, "Yes, we call it Nairmanika, and it remains well-preserved within a cave beneath the ocean's depths."

Akash kept asking, "Did other life forms on your planet also undergo a similar process of evolution as your kind?" out of continued interest.

"No, only our species underwent this special evolutionary journey," Mauktik stated. "The majority of the Janatigs perished because they were unable to adjust to their new surroundings. Only two individuals, a male and a female, managed to survive and carry on their lineage as a result of being specifically affected by Nairmanika's supernatural abilities. Their intelligence also increased as they changed. Our planet had mostly recovered by then, and its rich variety of flora and wildlife had also flourished."

Mauktik continued her account, saying, "As our species continued to evolve, we delved into the pursuit of knowledge and embarked on extensive research endeavours. We possessed ancient writings from our forebears, although these texts were not well-structured, and we grappled with rudimentary forms of communication. During that period, we lacked a formal language and mainly relied on non-verbal gestures for interaction."

She went on to describe a critical time in the history of her world, saying, "Approximately 3000 earth years ago, a mysterious traveller suddenly appeared on our planet. No one among our species had any idea where he came from or how he got there, but he claimed to be from earth. He had no trouble acclimating to our environment because he could breathe oxygen. This visitor became a great source of information for our forefathers, not only introducing them to the concept of earth but also to your language, Sanskrit. Because of its inherent values, our culture gradually adopted Sanskrit as our preferred form of verbal communication."

"Tragically, this earthly visitor succumbed to an incurable disease that was previously unknown to our kind," she narrated a sad episode in their history. "This loss had a significant impact on us. As time passed, our forefathers' interest in distant worlds and the cosmos beyond our globe rose rapidly. They wanted to know more about earth and its place in the vastness of the universe."

Mauktik then shifted her focus to a specific historical figure, saying, "Around 650 earth years ago, my great-great-grandfather, Avan, emerged as one of the brightest minds of his era. As Avan grew older, his curiosity about Nairmanika grew stronger, prompting him to explore the seemingly limitless possibilities that controlling its power would open up. His intense curiosity stretched to the worlds of outer space, and he was unwavering in his goal to find earth. Avan's outstanding performance and impressive achievements in the scientific and technical sectors culminated in his appointment as department head. He committed his life to developing unique products and technologies that improve our efficiency in numerous aspects of life. As his attention shifted to Nairmanika, Avan created a specialised scanner to decipher the composition of this intriguing crystal.

One day, with no prior notification to anyone, he embarked on an unauthorised expedition to the depths of the ocean, venturing into the cave where Nairmanika rested in its natural state. He set out to reveal the crystal's elemental makeup using his brilliant scanner. However, his attempt to remove a tiny piece from the enormous crystal brought about an unanticipated disaster. Avan accidentally triggered a luminous reaction by focusing a powerful laser beam on a tiny protruding edge of the dark purple crystal's surface, which eventually started glowing and suddenly released a massive surge of energy that resonated like an underwater explosion. The shockwaves spread over the entire ocean and neighbouring regions, warning everyone that a dreadful disaster was about to occur. Our island home saw tsunamis as a result of these shockwaves. Avan was thrown off by the blast's power and became unconscious. He awoke some 6 hours later in the same cave. As soon as Avan regained consciousness, he checked his scanner, which had miraculously survived, and found a sizeable gamma-ray burst signature. He next focused on Nairmanika, which, though no longer glowing, had a tiny, dazzling fragment break free from its enormous crystalline structure.

Avan made the decision to keep the specifics of his experiment a secret after arriving back on the island. He believed that if his fellow Janatigs had known the real source of the tsunami, they would have rejected any additional trials or research into it. A month or so after the terrible incident, Avan started to detect significant changes in his own capabilities and physical characteristics. He experienced a constant surge of energy that reduced his need for sleep and, on occasion, allowed him to go without it for 2 to 3 days in a row. He had significantly improved his physical ability, making him more fluid and agile than ever. It's interesting to note that his intellectual prowess had improved as well, inspiring him to come up with a ton of amazing discoveries and ground-breaking inventions.

Avan's renown rose as a result of his lifelong dedication to the study of Nairmanika and the search for earth's location. Younger Janatigs gravitated around him, inspired by his extraordinary achievements and ready to learn from him and help him carry on his legacy. Over time, this group of bright minds came together to form a powerful team. Avan discovered two unique kinds of matter when he was about 45 earth years old: one that interacted visibly inside our perceptible world, which you refer to as baryonic matter, and another that was outside the range of visibility, immersed in higher dimensions, and beyond the range of ordinary perception, which you have termed dark matter. Avan subsequently devised a tool that made it possible to access this ethereal, invisible material after many fruitless attempts. Furthering his study of this invisible exotic matter, he created a specialised suit that gave him the ability to teleport, allowing him to cover great distances in a matter of seconds.

Avan's life, however, was marked by a strange mystery. Under severe emotional strain, he saw that he had released a strange power that eluded his control and caused devastation in its immediate surroundings. This symptom usually appears in cases of frustration from unsuccessful experiments. However, his unrelenting curiosity and unfettered desire kept him moving forward in his quest for knowledge. Avan cautiously carried out his experiments in a secluded place far from civilisation, making sure that his companions were never put through any anxiety or discomfort from the potential consequences of his research. He started the creation of remote satellites and spacecraft in order to further understand the universe, working alongside a group of 12

Janatigs. Approximately 5780 people made up the Janatig population at that time."

Akash couldn't help but ask the inquiry after developing an inquisitive expression. "How," he wondered, "is it that after all this time, your population is still so small?"

Mauktik answered calmly, offering her opinion on the situation. She said in a controlled tone, "There are two main factors leading to our very low population. First off, among our species, ovulation occurs in females only once every 3 earth years, and even then, it only lasts for 3 days. I assume you are aware of what ovulation is."

The boys blushed involuntarily as a result of her sight, while Akash nodded in agreement.

"The second reason can be attributed to the governing body that creates and upholds our laws and regulations," Mauktik stated. "We all live on a huge island that has way too much room for up to 100,000 people to live comfortably. Our governing body is adamant that an excessively large population would make it extremely difficult for a single authority to govern. Additionally, they assert that such an event can result in the establishment of several groups within our society. We therefore work hard to maintain a sense of cohesion that is comparable to that of a huge family. 9644 people make up our current population."

In his response, Akash summed up his feelings about the situation in one word: "Fascinating."

Mauktik continued to narrate. "In order to learn more about earth, Avan studied everything he could from the human's remains as he continued his journey. Then, all of a sudden, he vanished. For months, no one was aware of his location; eventually, they discovered his covert research facility, but there was no sign of him. After around 900 days, he came back and told everyone everything."

Aditya was intrigued and felt the need to inquire, "So, where did he venture?"

With a contemplative face, Mauktik started to describe Avan's remarkable voyage. She said, "Avan's search for earth began right here within Ganagrah. As he dug more into his research on humans, he learned that the earthly traveller had come directly to our planet from earth. He came to the conclusion that there must be a means to travel from Ganagrah to earth as a result of this revelation. He set off on a long voyage, using teleportation to travel across different places and constantly improving his teleportation suit. He would relocate to random places on the planet for a while, meticulously cross-referencing human information with his calculations."

"Finally, after a thorough investigation, he discovered a spot where his estimates were accurate to a startling 99.9998%, reflecting the possibility of finding a cosmic tunnel," continued Mauktik. "He built a small research lab there after realising the importance of this discovery and committing himself to experimentation. A fortunate accident happened while testing the tiny piece of Nairmanika. Unexpectedly,

Avan discovered the presence of a primordial cosmic tunnel in our binary system that was around 2050000 times as large as our planet, whose gravitational waves highly interacted with Nairmanika's energy signature. He wasn't sure if this discovery was a stroke of luck or just a coincidence, but he had a deep-seated belief that this primordial tunnel was his route to earth. Avan, who was eager to set off on his quest, carefully calculated the 7.2 billion kilometres that separated Ganagrah from the primordial tunnel."

"He had substantially improved the capabilities of his teleportation suit in the interim, achieving a speed of 4200 km/s," she said after pausing for dramatic effect. "Additionally, he had added specific features to his suit to make travel through space smoother. He finally arrived at the target after almost 20 days of nonstop propulsion, only to find that the tunnel had absorbed enough mass and energy to create a portal to another universe. Avan took advantage of the opportunity and used his newly acquired advantage to reach the tunnel's opening just in time to be immediately sucked into its mysterious depths."

Mauktik continued to describe the events, giving the story more specifics. "A peculiar sensation gripped him as he entered the tunnel, causing him to lose consciousness. When he finally opened his eyes, he was covered in dirt, confused, and resting in a depression resembling a crater. His vision appeared blurry in the beginning, but clarity gradually returned. Avan's vision became clearer as he came to the startling conclusion that his risky experiment had in fact been successful. The beings staring at him with wonder and trepidation were none other than humans. Avan didn't give in to panic or confusion; he kept his cool. He could see that the depression where he was lying was the result of his collision with the earth's surface, and he surmised that everyone around him was probably talking about his unexpected landing from a high altitude."

Arjun interrupted with a pertinent query, as though unable to control his pique. "So, how is it that he was able to survive the fall from such a great height?"

The wise Mauktik replied, "You see, our physiology differs greatly from that of humans. Our skin is considerably thicker and more resilient, allowing it to withstand substantial shocks and injuries. In addition, we have a much higher threshold for pain than humans do."

With an understanding nod, Arjun took in the information, finding the answer to his initial question.

Mauktik continued, adding more specifics to the story as it was developing. "As I was saying, when he made his first attempts to engage with the crowd, chaos broke out, leading to wild yells and fast escapes. A calm rishi wearing saffron robes with flowing hair, a full beard, and a string of prayer beads in his palm stood out among the pandemonium, though. His forehead bore the marks of sacred ash.

This wise man came up to Avan and offered a hand, leading him away from the noisy crowd to a more private area. Avan felt an unexplainable sense of trust and connection when he spoke with the rishi. He shared the entirety of his travels because he had a sneaking suspicion that this sage was already aware of his kind. The rishi, on the other hand, showed no surprise at the astonishing narrative and remained unruffled by Avan's revelations. The rishi disclosed that he himself was on a great spiritual journey to the Himalay in order to discover and realise his purpose for being. Avan was greatly intrigued by this and, feeling a bond of kinship and trust with the sage, made the decision to go with him. Avan joined the rishi on this new voyage because he had no obvious way to return to his own house. Together, they travelled for days, climbing the snow-covered Himalayan summits and paying respects to the magnificent Namah Parvat along the route. The rishi felt an unexplainable calling upon reaching this holy summit—an inner beckoning leading him in a certain direction. He continued on his journey, propelled by this instinctive power, and soon found a fascinating forest. They came across another eminent sage who would show them the way to Jnañā-sthan here. Avan came to understand that only a human could be influenced or subconsciously guided towards the enigmatic realm of Jnañā-sthan."

"Do you mean to say that you had to follow us because you knew we would be guided to arrive here?" Aditya asked.

"Indeed, you are right," Mauktik said with a pleasant smile on her face.

Akash questioned, "The dog that guided us... was leading us here, wasn't it?" with a sense of awareness.

Again smiling and nodding in agreement, Mauktik said, "Yes, exactly."

Arjun said, "So, technically, we were compelled to come here!"

Mauktik responded, "On the contrary, there must be a profound reason why the three of you were picked to escort me here. I embrace the curiosity that binds you all. I'm just as interested in this as you are. However, it must bear enormous significance given Brahmarishi's desire for you to understand more about us."

Following a brief pause, Mauktik resumed her story: "Avan was completely enthralled by every facet of Jnañā-sthan, finding delight in every small detail. He had the honour of meeting Brahmarishi and shared his burning desire to discover the secrets of the cosmos and Nairmanika."

Again asking questions, Arjun yelled, "Wait, he met Brahmarishi then? He must not be that old."

Mauktik said after pausing for a while, "Truly, Brahmarishi is older than you can think. He and everyone else living here are immortal. A human needs to dedicate their entire existence to the voyage in order to get here; this involves steadfast commitment, unyielding determination, years of meditation bereft of earthly pleasures, and, above all, an unshakeable faith."

"Brahmarishi was delighted to encounter Avan, as it was the first time he had met a Janatig," Mauktik said in her tale.

"As Avan and Brahmarishi conversed in depth, he began to feel as though this was the place where he genuinely belonged—a place where he might discover his true self and solve the riddles of the cosmos. He admitted to Brahmarishi that he had spent his entire life trying to manage and use his miraculous abilities but had never been able to do so. Avan also expressed his sincere wish to learn more about Jnañā-sthan and discover how he might go back and forth between Ganagrah as necessary.

Avan's quest continued as he committed himself to learning from Brahmarishi and practiced strict meditation. He eventually managed to calm his restless thinking and aggressive attitude. He gradually became more interested in the study of chakras as he realised how crucial they were in gaining complete control over both himself and his environment, as well as in adopting the moral values of their society. Avan made the decision to leave Jnañā-sthan and go back to Ganagrah after a nearly 600-day extended stay, during which he improved his control of the chakras and utilised his special abilities.

On the day prior to his departure from Jnañā-sthan, Brahmarishi summoned Avan early in the morning. Avan hurried to meet the guru, who stressed the significance of delivering critical knowledge before Avan's return to Ganagrah. Brahmarishi revealed that a looming threat was approaching Ganagrah, drawn by the irresistible allure of Nairmanika, and it was imperative to safeguard this precious resource at any cost. 'It appears that your experimentation with Nairmanika has sent out an energy signal that resonated throughout the universe, piqueing the curiosity of certain entities who now seek to acquire it,' he said solemnly.

Brahmarishi did not go into specifics, but he did state that they should anticipate an approaching attack on Ganagrah and make the required preparations. Surprisingly, Avan's disposition has changed dramatically during his stay in Jnañā-sthan. Rather than becoming anxious, he stayed calm in the face of this foreboding news. Avan knelt before Brahmarishi, humbly bowing and pressing his brow to the sage's feet as he sought his blessings. He bid Brahmarishi farewell with a sorrowful heart and was led to the Gateway to Beyond, a gateway that could take him to any location inside the vast 7-universe cluster. He awoke in the realm of Ganagrah after passing through the Gateway to Beyond.

The people of Ganagrah had already mourned Avan's apparent death; hence, when he returned, their shock at his reappearance was palpable. Everyone was astonished by his new demeanour, which was characterised by courtesy and a steady perception of calm. Avan described his amazing journey to earth and the adventures he had experienced while living there. His legitimacy was initially questioned, but it was later supported by the many incredible achievements he had already achieved. Avan decided to build a Gurukul, a centre for learning, where he could share the knowledge and insight he had gained during his time spent in Jnañā-sthan. This choice was made in the days that followed. He rose to a significant position as one of the four important figures in the ruling body as his reputation developed. Avan made a ground-breaking suggestion, inviting everyone to visit his Gurukul for the benefit of all. By igniting all chakras, this endeavour helped individuals grow personally and cultivate a sense of serenity. Avan also vehemently promoted involvement in the development of cutting-edge technology.

Avan took the initiative to organise a dedicated team of robust individuals after seeing the need for defence. To get ready for impending dangers, he hired the most formidable Janatig as a coach and trainer. Avan rose to the highest levels of authority as time went on. His revolutionary choices and deeds altered the way of life of Ganagrah's inhabitants and considerably improved the planet's general wellbeing."

"He lived for 75,241 days," Mauktik revealed.

Arjun questioned, "Years?" after becoming perplexed.

"No, days," Mauktik said. "Like I already stated, our idea of time differs greatly from that of earth. In Ganagrah, a year is around 39,420 days; hence, we usually refer to a time in terms of days. Avan lived for approximately 206 earth years."

Obviously pleased, Arjun said, "Your math is quite fast."

"Following Avan's passing, we made an effort to preserve his brain and maintain his consciousness," Mauktik said with a pleasant smile. "His committed team set out on an ambitious project to connect his brain to a quantum computer."

"Like a robot?" Aditya asked.

"Not exactly a robot, but rather a colossal, living computing system ensconced within a highly secure vault," Mauktik clarified. "Prajñā was the name given to this research institution. It was one of our most amazing creations because it not only allowed Avan to remain with us but also served as a device that could answer almost any question or problem. It was able to handle our technology, watch over distant satellites, control our defensive systems, and predict future events. Importantly, it helped warn us of seismic activity, prevent possible disasters, and even assist in deflecting two impending asteroids away from our planet."

Mauktik's story proceeded, providing a vivid picture of the ages that passed. "The torch of duty was passed down to future generations, and Avan's grandson, Jaitra, carved out an outstanding career for himself, following in his grandfather's distinguished footsteps. Jaitra possessed tremendous strength as a result of the extraordinary qualities that had run through Avan's genetics, making him one of the most formidable Janatigs to grace our realm. He advanced to the position of chief of the defence group, delivering priceless tactical information to his compatriots, refined by his bright engineering mind. During his time in the defence unit, Jaitra found love in one of his coworkers, and after about 400 days of married bliss, the prophetic machine gave an unexpected insight while they both were working at the Prajñā facility. It was predicted that Jaitra and his wife would be gifted with triplets who would carry on Avan and Jaitra's legacy, excelling in every possible field and surpassing their forefathers' achievements. Above all, these three children would take on the responsibility of protecting Ganagrah from an enormously powerful external threat—an oncoming conflict that would mark the Janatigs' first war and would require thorough preparation. This prophecy, which spread like wildfire, caused some concern among the Janatigs at first. Despite this, they had faith in these unborn warriors because of the exceptional lineage from which they descended. Jaitra and his wife celebrated the birth of their triplets—three males named Ashvath, Atulya, and Achyut—nearly a decade later (using the earthly term of 3,652 days, modified to Janatig time)."

Mauktik continued her story, focusing on the three extraordinary siblings. "After their auspicious birth, their world was filled with excitement. But it didn't take long for the trio to become well-known. When they turned 500 days old, their parents brought them along while they were busy with other tasks at the Prajñā facility. During this visit, a coworker casually asked Prajñā which of the 3 kids would eventually aspire to be the greatest. To everyone's surprise, Prajñā quickly replied, designating Achyut as the chosen one. Yet the trio continued to receive equal love and attention; the prophecy had little impact on how they were treated.

The young Janatigs started their educational journey at the Gurukul as they grew older. They began a rigorous 3,000-day meditation routine throughout their formative years in order to awaken their chakras. Contrary to Prajñā's expectations, Achyut unexpectedly showed signs of being the least strong and sluggish of his siblings. Even though the forecast had never been wrong before, this deviation raised questions about Prajñā's invincibility. Compared to his brothers, Achyut needed an extra 600 days to awaken all of his chakras. He found it difficult to match Ashvath and Atulya's intellect in his many academic endeavours. Even though Achyut showed some skills resembling those of their ancestors, their might was meagre in contrast. On the other hand, Ashvath and Atulya stunned everyone with their superior abilities, boasting superior speed, agility, power, and strength.

As time passed, Achyut's difficulties continued, while Ashvath and Atulya engraved their names in Janatig history. Ashvath and Atulya succeeded to the position of leaders within the defence after officially obtaining senior rank after 6,940 days of hard work, succeeding their father. Meanwhile, Achyut found himself completely excluded from the defence. Among the joyous celebrations for Ashvath and Atulya's accomplishments, Achyut's presence was frequently overlooked, and doubt about Prajñā's prophecy grew."

"In the middle of these upheavals, Achyut mysteriously vanished. His brothers, Ashvath and Atulya, assembled their entire defence squad to look for him, using advanced equipment and satellites, but to no effect. For a long time, Achyut remained unidentified, with no indication of his location. However, after a considerable amount of time had elapsed, word regarding Achyut began to circulate throughout the community.

After around 100 days of searching, it seemed like all of the efforts had been in vain, and Achyut had vanished into obscurity. While still greatly mourning their brother, Ashvath and Atulya gradually accepted the circumstances and went back to their normal lives. Sometimes later, Ashvath fell in love with Iksha, and the two made the decision to get married. It was a significant occasion since it celebrated the marriage of their chief, and it gave the neighbourhood a lot of happiness.

A new chapter began when I was born into their world after 720 days of blissful wedlock. The following 200 days passed as life went on and people's memories of Prajñā's alarming prediction started to become less prominent. However, the moment the space radar picked up a strange occurrence, this sense of calmness was immediately broken. Concerns were raised by an unusual increase in the number of asteroids and asteroids-like objects in a nearby star system. Janatigs kept a close eye on the star system but discovered no reason for concern right away.

A little over 400 days later, on what appeared to be an ordinary night, the alarms started going off. Space-tech-specialised Janatigs watched with rising dread as hundreds of asteroid-like objects raced towards our planet from all sides."

Chapter 10:

The Great Battle of Ganagrah

As night fell, throwing a shadow over the area, just a few distant diyas lit the surroundings. However, the space beneath the towering banyan tree remained vividly lit by the dazzling glow originating from Mauktik's head, where she continued to tell her story.

"The Space Tech team quickly scanned the space surrounding our planet, covering millions of kilometres in all directions. Their studies revealed that the oncoming asteroids, which were now only 6 million kilometres away, were racing towards Ganagrah at a rate that would bring them dangerously close in 3 days. The space technology crew remained vigilant at all times, painstakingly tracking the movement and trajectory of approaching asteroids.

The mysterious and possibly worrisome threat was immediately communicated to the Defence Chiefs, Ashvath and Atulya. They immediately ordered the turn-on of all defence technology systems that were at their disposal and mobilised the remainder of the defence team. Despite being confined to a small island as our territory, our planet has a vast network of technological devices. These devices had the amazing capacity to create an invisible energy barrier that rose 300 kilometres above the surface of the Ganagrah.

This barrier was made up of two unique layers: an exterior layer that resembled a hexagonal prism and an even more powerful inner layer that was shaped like a sphere. Only 1450 people made up our defensive squad at that crucial time, equally split between males and females. Everyone in our kind gained some combat experience while being in Gurukul, so they could all pitch in when necessary.

Together with the Space Tech team, Ashvath and Atulya kept a constant watchful eye on the movement and trajectory of the approaching asteroids.

Over the course of the next 46 hours, these celestial intruders closed the distance to our planet significantly. The space technology team attempted to establish communication by sending signals, but there was no response from the approaching objects. The Defence Chiefs wisely refrained from launching any preemptive attacks until they could decipher the intentions behind this celestial conjunction.

Interestingly, the majority of these asteroids started to group together and form an odd cluster right above our island at a distance beyond the invisible barriers. This confusing assembly lasted for a while before abruptly changing. Several of these cosmic objects fell directly into the atmosphere of our planet. The outer energy barrier was struck, and a huge explosion followed. The barrier was momentarily made visible by the collision's impact, which caused it to emit a magnificent light. The ensuing shockwave rippled uniformly through the hexagonal prism.

Our chiefs, recognising the impending threat, promptly alerted the entire team to stand ready. The onlookers experienced a wave of terror as they observed an unexpected incident. Following the initial bombardment, the once-converged asteroids dispersed into the spatial vicinity, aligning near one of the prism's corners that got exposed due to the initial bombardment. The hail of asteroids continued there for several ferocious minutes, concentrated at that specific juncture. When the bombardment finally stopped, it was clear that the persistent attack had damaged the energy barrier's corner, causing a gaping hole in it. Subsequently, more asteroids began to amass at this weakened point, poised for an additional strike.

Such behaviour from celestial bodies was an unprecedented spectacle, suggesting a level of control and intentionality far beyond anything we had previously encountered. The entire unfolding drama was closely monitored from our research centre. All across our island, laser guns sprang to life, their beams piercing the sky as we focused our efforts on targeting the incoming asteroids that breached the damaged section of the barrier. Simultaneously, we supercharged the inner energy barrier, heightening its defence capabilities.

Our laser weapons were successful in intercepting and destroying a large number of these cosmic intruders. Fortunately, any asteroid striking the inner barrier was instantly crushed to a fine, harmless dust, giving us what appeared to be a temporary advantage. This hope, however, was short-lived as far larger, ominous-looking asteroids started to appear seemingly out of nowhere. These enormous things joined the continuous drop and passed through the compromised section of the barrier.

When these mammoth asteroids collided with the inner barrier, they disintegrated like their smaller counterparts but appeared to be considerably denser. The subsequent dust cloud gathered on the barrier's surface, generating an increasing amount of heat that gradually began to melt the protective membrane of the inner barrier. As the dust accumulated, it became reddish-orange incandescent, indicating the rising intensity of the barrier's destruction. This onslaught of cosmic invaders showed no signs of abating, collecting on the barrier's surface and steadily eroding a significant chunk of it. The ensuing damage to the barrier covered about a square kilometre, indicating a large and worrying breach in our defences.

Our world was exposed in the face of these mysterious intrusions. Only a few hundred tiny asteroids were left floating above the huge breach in the outer barrier, suggesting that they had significantly exhausted the entire asteroid cluster. Both the asteroids' descent and our laser cannons' shooting temporarily ceased as a peculiar silence descended over the scene. Then, in front of us, a remarkable sight appeared. We observed a sleek, elongated, and bright black ellipsoid passing through the opening in the barrier. The smaller asteroid-like formations were orbiting this ellipsoid, giving the impression of artificial gravity. We got a better look at the objects in tow as this ellipsoid passed past the second energy barrier. Strikingly, these objects did not resemble conventional asteroids; instead, they bore the hallmarks of artificial creations.

We resumed our laser assault on the black ellipsoid in response. The smaller asteroids that circled it nevertheless served as a shield. These shielding asteroids shattered upon impact, revealing an unexpected discovery: creatures, or rather, robots, emerged from their interiors. These mechanical beings made a measured descent and landed on the shore of our island. Our monitoring systems went into overdrive in response to this unexpected development, carefully examining the unfolding events. There was a recognisable pattern of behaviour among the robotic entities that had left the protected asteroids as if they were all running on a common program. Their metallic bodies were made of a previously unidentified substance that had an extraordinarily high density, adding to the mystery surrounding their origins and motivations.

As the robots advanced towards our city, our defence leaders quickly issued orders to our crew to prepare for conflict. After destroying all of the asteroids orbiting the ellipsoid shuttle, our laser weapons quickly altered their targeting, focusing their beams on the robots. Another cannon that had been aiming at the ellipsoid shuttle for a while finally hit its target and brought the craft down.

In the middle of the pandemonium, Ashvath directed Atulya to explore the shuttle's wreckage, fearing that the mastermind behind the attack could be located within. In the meantime, he stayed on the battlefield, directing and battling with our defence troops. The clash between the two troops erupted into violent combat, blazing the battlefield with a hail of laser fire. Despite being outnumbered, we were able to hold our own against the robotic invaders because of our tenacity and training.

In a hurried attempt to identify the perpetrator of this attack, Atulya went to the wrecked shuttle. He forced the top shell of the shuttle open with his strong, muscular arms, only to be shocked by the discovery that there were no beings within. Instead, there was no room for a pilot; it was instead home to a complex network of equipment. In response to this puzzling revelation, Atulya immediately issued orders to our space technology experts and Prajñā researchers. They were tasked with conducting an exhaustive planetary scan, even utilising our network of satellites, to ensure that no hidden threats were lurking or attempting to flee our world. With this precaution in place, Atulya re-joined his brother and the rest of the team on the battlefield, ready to continue the fight against the robotic invaders."

Mauktik then fell silent for a brief while, creating a buzz among the audience. "What happened?" Akash couldn't help but wonder.

Her initial response was evasive: "Nothing!" She then altered her tone and resumed her story.

Returning to her tale, she recalled flashes of vivid, colourful light emanating from the battlefield at that point. "After an hour of hard combat, the Janatigs had dismantled a quarter of the robotic army with no casualties on their side. The combat, however, took an unexpected turn when the deactivated parts of the defeated robots were absorbed and merged by the still-active ones, increasing their power.

Following the elimination of nearly half of the robotic foes, an unexpected development occurred in the conflict: the robots stopped attacking the Janatigs and started congregating in one place. The Janatig team carefully responded by stopping their attack while continuing to watch out for the robots' possible next moves. To their astonishment, the robots began to combine, forming larger and larger clusters until they finally came together to form a massive robot of immense proportions, standing as tall as an eight-story building. This enormous creature started moving relentlessly towards the centre of the city.

The massive robot loomed enormous, resistant to the barrage of lasers and bullets raining down on it. The Janatigs were confused and unsure of how to deal with this tremendous menace since these attacks seemed to be absorbed with ease.

The defence leaders worked nonstop to find any vulnerability in the big robot's defences that might be used against them. In this dire situation, Atulya appealed to the Prajñā researchers, pleading with them to do a thorough scan of the massive foe in the hopes of identifying a weakness. After some anxious waiting, the researchers reported their findings: they had discovered a significant energy source close to the giant robot's left shoulder, one whose energy signature was so strong that neutralising it might provide a means of victory. With this crucial knowledge in hand, Atulya and Ashvath devised a strategy to defeat the behemoth.

They commanded their defence squad to continue their unrelenting assault on the robot, drawing its attention and keeping it focused on them. Ashvath and Atulya would sneak up on the energy source and neutralise it while doing so. The two brothers ventured to the back of the robot in search of a suitable point of entry as the defence team's assault continued, creating a distraction. They prepared their attack after spotting a weak spot close to the energy source. Ashvath leapt into the air while wielding a powerful electric blade. Ashvath was assisted with an even bigger leap thanks to Atulya's tremendous power, which propelled him even higher into the air. Ashvath quickly cut through the robot's protective coating as he dropped on its left shoulder with accuracy and tenacity. As they landed on the ground, Ashvath and Atulya gazed upon the partially exposed energy source—a miniature, star-like, bright structure intricately connected to the robot's body by millions of thin fibre-like wires through an outer socket containing the energy source.

Ashvath signalled for Atulya to join him, and the two brothers, ready for the mission at hand, launched another enormous leap, charging with determination towards the vital energy source."

Mauktik paused once more, her face mirroring the feelings that were now reflecting from her eyes—a sight that the three young listeners had not missed.

Arjun inquired about her wellbeing out of genuine care.

In a composed yet hesitant manner, Mauktik responded with a "Yes."

Akash wanted to hear what happened after this fierce battle, so he asked, "What happened next? Did your father and your group win the battle?"

Mauktik took a deep breath and began to recount the events that had transpired. "Yes," she said, "but at a tremendous cost. That day etched memories in our hearts that continue to haunt us even now. As they charged towards the power source with determination, a voice suddenly echoed through the wireless talker, shouting 'No...,' and then, in the blink of an eye, a colossal explosion rocked the battlefield."

Her description of the mayhem that followed—a brilliant flash of light, a deafening boom, followed by a shockwave that swept the region—was unforgettable. "When the survivors were finally able to regain vision and stand up, the enormous robot was still, its massive frame crumbling into pieces that gradually fell from the sky.

The defensive team, although victorious, soon realised that their chiefs, Ashvath and Atulya, were missing. They used their talker to try and get in touch with them, but no one answered. An early feeling of triumph was quickly replaced by fear as the leaders went missing. The team scoured the area, searching for any trace of Ashvath and Atulya, but their efforts proved futile. After approximately half an hour of frantic searching, a call rang out, summoning the team to the nearby beach. Gathered there, they were met with a heartbreaking sight—two lifeless, charred bodies lay near the shore, about a kilometre from the blast's epicentre.

Desperate to ensure the wellbeing of their chiefs, they rushed to their side, but there was no sign of life. The shocking news soon spread among them, and grief overcame the entire group. It marked the first time in our history that two of our own had met an unnatural end. My father and my uncle's deaths filled our home and life with an overpowering sense of emptiness. As I grew up and gained a deeper understanding of our circumstances, I made the choice to join the defence group, following the footsteps of my father and uncle. It remains a dark event in our history to this day."

Mauktik continued, diving deeper into the events of that fateful day. "By the end of the day," she recalled, "all of the alien incursion's remnants, including the ellipsoid shuttle, had been gathered and transported to our research laboratory. Ashvath and Atulya's lifeless bodies were also brought into the lab for a comprehensive inspection."

She described how their dead leaders' remains were meticulously kept after being examined. They were placed in glass chambers and enclosed in ice slabs the size of coffins. Then, at the identical spots where the victims had been found along the shore, these chambers were reverently buried deep below the land. The location was transformed into a holy and revered location, decorated to honour the memories of the two gallant leaders who had paid the ultimate price.

The intense suffering that had engulfed their community during those terrible times was acknowledged by Mauktik. The researchers painstakingly carried on their analysis of the items gathered from the foreign invasion as they grappled with their grief. She did, however, mention that their discoveries had been much more unexpected; very little of the alien robots had been recovered, almost as if the majority of their components had vanished in the enormous blast.

She continued, "After several days of diligent research, we started to understand these alien beings' amazing technological innovations. The ellipsoid shuttle gave off the impression that synthetic intelligence was guiding it because it was moving on its own without a pilot. The robots were built from a unique alloy that included a number of additional elements to produce a material with amazing density. This made the composition of the robots themselves much more intriguing. As we learned more about their technology, we came to see that it wasn't just a window into their culture but also a way to advance our own technological know-how.

With this newfound understanding, we were able to enhance and fix our defence-related, invisible barriers.

During this time of rehabilitation, Prajñā, our esteemed research facility, was crucial in understanding and expanding our technology. Days went by, and life on our planet gradually started to return to normal. But around 3500 days after the battle, Prajñā got a baffling communication from the farthest reaches of the cosmos. A terrifying prophecy with a warning of a much bigger and riskier threat lurking in our future was encoded in this communication. It was evident what this menacing entity wanted: Nairmanika, which we had to protect at all costs. A source of power from earth has to be collected in order to protect Nairmanika.

What struck us the most was the energy signature contained within the message, which was similar to the one recorded by Avan upon his return from earth and linked it to Jnañā-sthan, the location he had visited on his journey. This revelation further complicated the prophecy's ambiguous meaning by firmly suggesting a link between this impending peril and Jnañā-sthan."

Mauktik added, "The team endured a period of transformation after the devastating loss of our Defence Chiefs. With their spirits lifted by the legacy of my father and uncle, the new members brought a new feeling of zest and vitality to the group. Our training programme became substantially more rigorous, with difficult tasks carried out in dangerous situations to hone our resiliency.

I, too, joined the ranks of these newcomers, carrying the weight of my forefathers' legacies with me. I underwent arduous training for 4500 days and distinguished myself by winning multiple contests. I was ultimately chosen to be the one tasked with pursuing the prophecy by to earth because of this success.

After being selected, I had to endure an agonising wait of almost another 800 days for the cosmic portal that would be my route to earth. We used Prajñā's resources in addition to the intelligence Avan had left for us to use in our computations. When the time came for my voyage, I set out on my task with a steadfast determination to defend my home planet and its inhabitants from any potential threats. I've arrived here before you after going through a great deal of hardship."

Arjun remarked in awe, "Your race and everything about your world are truly remarkable."

Aditya extended his sorrow by expressing, "I'm deeply sorry to hear about the losses you've endured."

Akash was curious: "Have these threats returned since that battle?"

"Not yet, but the possibility still exists," Mauktik retorted. "Our investigation indicates that their major goal in the attack was probably to evaluate our technology and defences. They appear to have a substantial technological advantage over us, though. We have upgraded our technology in light of what we could discern from theirs, but we are unsure of the full scope of their developments."

"Do you have any knowledge about the specific powers you seek, which brought you here?" Arjun continued.

Mauktik acknowledged, "Not exactly. That is the main reason I came."

Brahmarishi joined them while they conversed and came up from behind. "I assume you've been informed about Ganagrah and its tragic history," he said, turning to the group.

"Yes," Akash responded.

Then Brahmarishi made the comment, "It's becoming late. I advise everyone to eat dinner and take a nap. Tomorrow, we can resume our conversation."

Mauktik was intrigued by the boys' role in her voyage, but she refrained from pressing Brahmarishi because he had already suggested that they continue their talk the next day. They all reunited in the same cabin, where they had lunch for supper. Mauktik then returned to her hut, while the boys lingered near their own before eventually entering it after some time.

The boys gradually awoke the next morning as the sun's rays gently filtered through their window. They got up one by one and went outdoors to get some fresh air. They believed Mauktik was awake because her hut's door was already ajar. Arjun decided to make the short stroll to the adjacent river stream to replenish their water supply after realising it was running low. As he reached the tranquil river, he noticed Mauktik, who was intensely absorbed in her meditation in a padmasan position by the river's edge. He continued with his duties without disturbing her.

On his way back, he lingered for a while, transfixed by Mauktik's peaceful visage, which appeared to glow even brighter in the early sunlight. With these thoughts, he returned to their hut, reflecting on how their experience with Mauktik had already changed their lives and what the future held for them.

Nishka entered after a while and greeted them with a traditional "Suprabhaatam," uniting her hands in a respectful gesture. The identical salutation was returned by the boys. She generously served them fruits and sweets for breakfast.

After finishing their breakfast, the guys went outside in search of Mauktik, anxious to discover more about the duration of their stay. They were elated when they saw Mauktik and Brahmarishi approaching from opposite directions.

"I hope you all had a good night's sleep," Brahmarishi inquired warmly.

Mauktik saluted him by joining her hands and saying, "Pranam Brahmarishi, Suprabhaatam." Following her lead, the boys exchanged respectful welcomes, and Aditya added, "Yes, we had a good sleep."

"I'm pleased to hear that," Brahmarishi answered, smiling.

Mauktik turned to Brahmarishi, her curiosity unabated, and asked, "Brahmarishi, I am still unclear about why they are here and their purpose in my journey."

"They are the individuals you seek," Brahmarishi said confidently. "These three boys, or Triansh, possess the power to safeguard Nairmanika."

"Excuse me, what are we again?" Arjun inquired, seeking clarification.

Brahmarishi stated unequivocally, "Triansh."

Chapter 11:

Triansh

A profound silence enveloped everyone present as Brahmarishi unveiled the term "Triansh." Even Mauktik herself appeared baffled by this revelation. After a brief pause, Aditya broke the silence with a question: "What is Triansh?"

"Triansh was the affectionate nickname given to the three brothers during their youth by the Janatigs, shortly after Prajñā made its prophecy about them," Mauktik said after clearing her throat. "People expected these three to usher in prosperity and protect their race from all imaginable challenges, especially considering their ancestry goes back to Avan. However, as the years passed, Achyut failed to live up to the expectations of the others and eventually vanished. The term Triansh vanished from recollection over time, and it was mostly linked with Ashvath and Atulya."

"So, Brahmarishi thinks we are Triansh?" Arjun questioned.

The boys exchanged pale looks before bursting into laughter. Their behaviour, however, did not sit well with

Mauktik, who sported a small frown. Her confusion at Brahmarishi's remarks lingered, and she couldn't help but ask, "Brahmarishi, I beg your pardon, but how can they be considered Triansh? They are only human beings. How are they going to safeguard us and Nairmanika? They appear to be too fragile for such a duty. They'd have no chance against the menace we've already faced."

Akash interjected, "Hey, that was harsh," and Arjun added, "But true." A moment of contemplative silence followed.

Brahmarishi responded, "I assume you are familiar with the life cycle of the Janatig." Mauktik replied, "Of course, Brahmarishi."

Aditya inquired, "What does that mean?" Mauktik explained, "I suppose you might be aware that every living body has a soul, and when the mortal body dies, the soul departs from the physical remains and seeks a new body in a continuous cycle. The same holds true for us as well."

Aditya responded with disbelief, "Are you serious? Do your people genuinely believe in souls and spirits? I thought you were such an advanced species to believe in such things."

Mauktik replied, "Well, indeed, we do. Every living body is intrinsically connected to a soul. A soul represents a form of cosmic energy that bestows consciousness on us. This is how we perceive our profound connection with the universe."

Aditya expressed his scepticism, saying, "Well, your stories were fascinating at first, but now I'm becoming bored. As a science student, I find it difficult to believe in things that cannot be empirically proven."

Mauktik responded, "Certainly, it can be proven. However, I'm afraid I don't have the time to delve into such matters right now. Brahmarishi, you were saying..."

"Excuse me, I have a small question if you don't mind," Arjun said, interrupting with a query. With a little haste, Mauktik said, "Okay, go ahead."

Arjun questioned, "How does the population grow if the circle of life continues with a soul from one life to another? Let's imagine two or more babies are born at the same time when one person passes away. The spirit of the deceased is given to one of the newborns, but what about the others? What is the source of their souls?"

"Well, that's a great question," Mauktik said with more explanation. "Our ancestors realised the importance of keeping our spirits safe within our community. We needed to protect our souls within our community since the powers that we have received from Nairmanika also have an impact on them. We intend to infuse new life into our community when one of us is on the verge of death. We normally give birth to two or more children at a time, unlike humans. We rarely have only one child among our species. We know roughly when a Janatig will pass away because we often die naturally. A couple decides to have a child in light of this. Because of the meticulous planning, the embryo starts to develop soon after someone passes away. Therefore, when a circumstance occurs where more than one progeny is intended to be created, the soul copies and divides, much like how cells divide. This custom has been practiced ever since we began."

Arjun retorted, "That sounds fair."

After a little pause, during which it looked like all of the questions had been answered, Brahmarishi continued, "So, as I was saying, when Prajñā made the prophecy regarding the foreign invasion, for some reason, it failed to convey another critical piece of information. It did not clarify that its heroes would perish unless the attack on Ganagrah was dealt with in a specific way, outside of the planet. So, an instant later, a series of events began to take place as Ashvath and Atulya moved to destroy the energy source. Ashvath and his brothers were killed when they neared their swords into the power source, which aggressively responded and unleashed a tremendous rush of energy. It started absorbing material from the robots' bodies at the same time. The energy source experienced a collapse as the heavy metals were drawn into it, creating an incredibly dense object with the ability to bend space-time. Gradually, this entity momentarily transformed into a cosmic tunnel. Even though it was small, it was incredibly powerful because it was trying to draw in as much matter and energy as it could. The three brothers were killed by a massive gamma-ray burst that was released as a result, and their souls were dragged into the cosmic tunnel. The explosion that followed expelled their dead bodies. On earth, the other end of this cosmic tunnel appeared, therefore transferring their souls into the new realm, but it was short-lived and quickly disappeared. All of these things happened in a fraction of a second."

"Brahmarishi, excuse my confusion, but did you mention that all three of the brothers perished in the blast?" Mauktik said. "There were only Ashvath and Atulya, for sure. Before I was even born, Achyut vanished and never surfaced again. Also, beyond Ashvath and Atulya's remains, we never found any others after the battle."

"I understand the common perception among Janatigs, but that's not entirely accurate," Brahmarishi retorted. "Achyut did come back and try to save his brothers, but sadly, they all perished. Following their souls' voyage into another universe, they encountered a different species that resembled the Janatigs. These three souls chose to begin new lives at the same time. Though located in different cities, within a few months, all three were born on the same day. Soon after, fate stepped in to bring them together. They were neighbours and developed a strong friendship early on, becoming actual brothers as they grew older."

Mauktik inquired, "So if I understand correctly, it means that my father, Atulya, and Achyut live inside these boys?" as she pointed towards the boys.

Brahmarishi confirmed, "That would be accurate."

Aditya proclaimed his doubt, adding, "You know, it's quite challenging for me to believe in all this talk of souls and reincarnation."

"But, Aditya, consider this: what Brahmarishi said about us seems to align with reality," Akash countered. "We are all the same age and have the same birthday. In addition, my parents and Arjun's parents relocated to our current house shortly after we were born. We've always had a close relationship that makes us feel as though we've known each other forever. We spent our entire childhood together, went to the same school, and were in the same class."

"Couldn't this simply be a coincidence?" Arjun wondered.

"It's possible," Akash said, "but there's another peculiar aspect. For a long time, my father tried to relocate to his hometown, and twice he almost succeeded, but it never happened."

Aditya remembered, "Yes, I remember that; you even had a farewell event in our class."

"In spite of the fact that returning after the farewell was a little embarrassing," Akash said, "from my perspective, it's genuinely strange how the three of us have always been together."

"True," Arjun said, "but it still seems like a mere coincidence to me."

"What are we supposed to do right now?" Aditya wondered as he turned to face Mauktik. "Go to your planet and get killed in no time."

"Hold on, do you guys really want to get entangled in all of this?" Arjun interjected, issuing a warning. "I've been genuinely afraid of everything we've gone through so far. And right now, you're actually thinking of visiting a different planet in a different universe?"

"Bro, calm down. There's no need to be alarmed," Aditya soothed. "No one's going anywhere. Listen to what they have to say first."

"I understand your worries; it does make me a little anxious too," Akash continued. "But if you think about it, it's also rather thrilling—journeying to another planet through space. Arjun, you used to be so excited about all this stuff. What's changed?"

"Have you lost your mind?" Arjun responded. "They're talking about a different universe here. Do you have any idea how vast that could be? We have families here. What about our parents?"

Aditya's eyes widened as he instantly recognised what it was, and he shouted, "Oh my gosh! Mom and dad! They must think we have passed away. We had been gone for such a very long time. By now, Sharad must have told them."

Panic spread across the boys' faces as they came to this realisation.

In order to speak alone with Brahmarishi, Mauktik wished to leave the chaos. She addressed the boys, saying, "Could you guys please excuse us for a moment?"

Mauktik and Brahmarishi moved a short distance away, and she inquired, "Brahmarishi, how can these humans assist us in facing such a threat? They can't last very long in our world. How can they protect Nairmanika and us from an unforeseen threat?"

The answer from Brahmarishi was, "It's only a matter of time. You'll understand everything eventually. Although it will be difficult, you must accept them as members of your own species. At that point, advancement will start. They also contain the souls of the most formidable Janatigs, which are dormant inside them right now. They will be prepared to travel to your planet once they are awakened. Regarding the ability to survive in your world, I think Janatigs have highly developed medical engineering and are able to integrate their old bodies with their new ones. Just a little patience with them will do. They are just young individuals, and with time, they will mature and understand."

"Okay, but do you think they'll leave everything behind here and travel with me to another world?" Mauktik retorted. "They already seem hesitant. Two of them appear firm in their decisions."

"It is their destiny to defend your people and your world," Brahmarishi informed her. "As I said, it's just a matter of time before everything comes together. It only takes a little patience."

"All right, Brahmarishi, as you intend," Mauktik retorted.

After their intense discussion ended, Brahmarishi and Mauktik re-joined the guys. The guys were confused and curious at the same time. "I understand that the past few days have been incredibly confusing for you three, and I have no right to compel you to accompany me," Mauktik stated to the guys. "However, I've learned that the fate of my planet and its inhabitants relies on you three. It is essential that you all accompany me to Ganagrah. I absolutely understand how challenging it is for you to depart from your house and your parents and travel to a new place. However, the current issue is more important than anything else. Countless lives will look to you once they discover that their saviours exist in a different form. I want you to give this decision some serious thought since I know how difficult it is." The boys' curiosity and confusion began to settle. Mauktik and Brahmarishi departed the scene after that.

"So, what do you all think about it?" Akash asked.

"What?" Arjun retorted. "Are you serious? We are not discussing anything further. I only know that we are returning home."

Akash persisted, saying, "Look, it's not that simple. We must also take into account their point of view. We are exactly what Brahmarishi said we were. Furthermore, there are still a great many unanswered questions. Not all events may be attributed to coincidence. On our journey, we had originally expected to be somewhere else, but fate has brought us here. I know a lot about the geography of our country, but I've never heard of Jnañā-sthan. We wouldn't have believed it if someone had told us about a place like this. We've wanted to trek Moksh Parvat for a long time, but I can't remember why we initially selected this particular trek. Therefore, it is clear that we are here to serve a purpose. In regard to our families, I presume they are already devastated, having likely received the news of our disappearance. I can't remember how many days have passed since we vanished. We may safely state that our parents have a pessimistic outlook. Personally, I think we should leave things as they are and focus on what lies ahead."

Aditya responded, "Well, I kind of agree with Akash. I think we should follow the flow if we are meant to be somewhere else and if our life's purpose includes helping their people. Let's see what they have planned for us next, and then we can make an informed decision."

Arjun, on the other hand, firmly objected, saying, "No, I can't go along with that. I have to stay with my family. To me, they are everything. Even if they believe I'm gone, I'm certain their joy will be immeasurable when they see me return."

With compassion, Akash said, "I get it, my brother. Try, nonetheless, to keep the big picture in mind. When given the responsibility of saving lives, we shouldn't back down from a worthy endeavour. Once our mission is complete, we can return to our home."

Aditya continued, "Yes, we might never get the chance to come back for this if we go home right now."

Arjun remained unwavering and said, "Nope, my decision stands."

"Then I suppose we'll be parting ways from here," Akash said in conclusion.

Everyone was briefly rendered speechless by the weight of Akash's statement. The fact that Arjun wouldn't be joining them in their joint pursuits for the first time was difficult for Akash and Aditya to accept.

The guys made their way away from each other, finding comfort in their seclusion as they thought about the enigmatic future that lay before them. Although they had collectively reached a decision about the path they would embark upon, a subtle undercurrent of uncertainty still swirled within each of them, casting doubt on the choices they had made. These lingering questions persisted in their minds, clouding their thoughts, and they couldn't help but wonder if their chosen course of action was actually the right one.

Evening settled on the quiet lakeside as the golden rays of the setting sun covered the surroundings. The three boys found themselves sitting at the water's edge, maintaining a thoughtful distance between them. In this peaceful time, they didn't say anything, allowing the sounds of nature to take centre stage and fill the air with their calming melodies.

The quiet was soon softly broken by the return of Brahmarishi and Mauktik to the boys' company. The three young men stood up when they spotted their mentors and went up to the two guests. Mauktik could see that the boys were suffering from their choice, and she couldn't help but join in with their solemn expression. She asked, "Have you arrived at your decisions, or do you feel that you need more time?" realising the seriousness of the decision they had to make.

Before Akash finally responded, the group of three exchanged wary looks. Akash then said, "Yes, Adi and I have chosen to accompany you on your quest, but Arjun has decided to return to his home." Arjun remained mute, making his decision clear.

"I assume you thoroughly thought this through before making your options," Mauktik said as she acknowledged their choices.

"Yes," Aditya replied.

"In that case, we should start getting ready for the next phase." Mauktik continued.

Akash was perplexed and said, "What do you mean by that?"

"You obviously can't just wander around on our planet like that," Mauktik said. "There may be oxygen shortages in some areas, but since we don't breathe oxygen, it doesn't concern us. You'll also need to undergo a procedure to adapt to our environment and harness our natural abilities."

Aditya shook his head and asked, "What kind of procedure?"

"It won't be especially uncomfortable, and you won't be totally conscious throughout the procedure," Mauktik informed. "However, before any of this takes place, you need to understand yourselves and your inner essence. To have control over your body, your organs, and most importantly, to awaken your spirit, you must become enlightened."

Akash asked for clarification: "How do we achieve that?"

Mauktik explained, "You will receive training here in Jnañā-sthan, guided by me under Brahmarishi's mentorship, much like how Avan was trained by Brahmarishi."

Together, Akash and Aditya spoke the word "okay.."

"What about me?" Arjun asked from behind in a cool, collected tone. "Can someone guide me on how to get home from here?"

"Certainly, my child," Brahmarishi replied. "But I'd advise you to think about living here for a bit. You can engage in learning the sadhnas alongside your friends. This will not only enhance your agility and resilience but also allow you to spend valuable time with your companions."

Arjun gave it some thought and realised that Brahmarishi's counsel was sound. Perhaps this was his last chance to be with Akash and Aditya, and he would inevitably return home afterward. Additionally, the potential to pick up new information and abilities now can come in handy later. In light of this, Arjun agreed and said, "Okay, I can stay here a little longer."

Aditya asked, "Okay, so where do we start? And when will we leave on our trip to Ganagrah after finishing this educational process?"

"Well, that entirely depends on you—how effectively you perform your tasks, how skilfully you can meditate, and how early you can activate the 9 chakras within your body," Brahmarishi retorted.

Akash asked, "What?" sounding a little astonished. "Are there 9 chakras? Only 7 have I heard of."

"To be precise, there are 12, but for now it's preferable to concentrate on achieving 9," Brahmarishi clarified with a smile. "If you try to accomplish all of them at once, you might find it difficult to complete any. The idea is to set more manageable, shorter goals. You can advance further to link with the Soul Star and Spirit chakras after successfully opening the Sahasrara chakra, often known as the seventh chakra. This should be sufficient for your journey to Ganagrah."

Akash questioned, "So, meditation is the means to attain these chakras?" in an effort to get more information.

"Meditation alone will not suffice," Brahmarishi explained. "You must go deep within yourself, become aware of your inner self, and connect with the universe. It will take time, but I am confident that every one of you will succeed."

Aditya was determined, saying, "I've never meditated before, but I'll give it my all. It is, after all, for the greater benefit."

Arjun strolled in silence behind the others, seeming less excited than the others. Mauktik, on the other hand, was unable to stop staring at each of the boys, her mind filled with the possibility that one of them might be her father. When Akash noticed Mauktik's thoughtful countenance, he asked, "Do you have anything on your mind?"

After a brief moment of surprise, Mauktik replied, "Yes, we must begin your training as soon as possible. Let's start tomorrow at an early hour because the day is coming to an end. We can't afford to wait much longer."

All three guys echoed the same response: "Understood."

Chapter 12:

Rising from the Ashes

Brahmarishi had entrusted Mauktik with the initial training of the boys, encompassing all the necessary skills they would require to thrive in Ganagrah. Both Brahmarishi and Mauktik noted that for the boys to begin their spiritual journey, they needed to alter their daily routines and develop self-discipline.

The next morning, the teenage boys awoke to the constant chirping of birds outside their window. They noticed that the sky had begun to light up, even though the sun had not yet risen above the horizon. They realised that this ambient light would act as their daily alarm. They awoke from their sleep and went about their morning rituals right away. When they saw the first rays of the sun, they followed Mauktik's earlier directions and went straight to the river.

The sun was steadily rising over the horizon as they got closer to the river. They noticed a large group of other saints gathered by the bank of the river, all getting ready for their morning ablutions. The boys' first foray into the chilly water was a bracing experience, but with time, they acclimated to the temperature and submerged their entire bodies.

They took several cleansing dips, prayed to the rising sun, and then got out of the water. They put on the spotless white dhotis that had been given to them and would be their attire for the duration of their stay in the ashram.

As they walked back to their hut, they couldn't help but notice that the door to Mauktik's house was still firmly locked. The boys looked at each other in confusion, thinking it odd that Mauktik was still dozing off. Just as they were on the verge of stepping inside their own hut, the door to Mauktik's residence creaked open, revealing Nishka as she emerged.

The guys were completely astounded by what they saw next. Someone, draped in a resplendent white saree with golden borders, gracefully exited Mauktik's abode. The overwhelming beauty of Mauktik's arrival rendered them speechless. She resembled an ethereal figure from the heavens and seemed to radiate an otherworldly beauty. The boys were rendered momentarily speechless by her enchanting presence.

Observing Akash and Aditya gazing in awe at Mauktik, Arjun playfully interjected, "Let's not forget, she's actually the daughter of one of us."

"I know, but just look at her," Akash retorted with a melancholy tone. "She's absolutely stunning. If she were my daughter, I'd be bursting with pride."

"Don't start to act like a father now," Aditya added with a smile. "Remember that technically you are younger than she is?"

Mauktik noticed the boys' return with a faint grin on her lips as she examined their attire. She couldn't help but smile as she saw the boys dressed in dhotis. The guys immediately quieted each other as she approached them to demonstrate their respect.

"Suprabhaatam," Mauktik greeted them heartily, and the guys returned the favour. "I am very delighted and pleased to see all three of you adopting our routines right from the first day," she said as she expressed her joy. "Let's eat breakfast first, and then we can start the day." With that, Mauktik retreated back, and the boys made their way into their hut.

The three left their cabin after finishing their breakfast to discover Mauktik waiting for them outside. She led them to a nearby open space where they would start their training. When the boys arrived, Mauktik instructed them to start running as quickly as they could, telling them to touch the far end of the open field and then come back. This exercise was followed by brief breaks.

She then assigned them the duty of climbing trees and jumping from heights they were comfortable with. The boys were physically exhausted as a result of these exercises, which lasted for a few hours. They cleaned themselves off and went back to their home around midday. Later that day, Mauktik started teaching lessons on the science and technology that they would require in Ganagrah. She even gave them problems based on actual situations to see how well they could solve them.

This tough programme lasted several days and was supplemented by morning yoga and meditation sessions. Their daily schedules began and ended with meditation, which played a special role in their curriculum. The young boys were expected to perform basic housekeeping duties, including cleaning their hut twice a day and washing their utensils, in addition to their instructions. They slept on mud floors, which at first seemed frightening to them because it was a very different way of living from what they were used to. They did, however, gradually get used to the entire process over time.

The boys needed more than a week to get used to their new way of life. After a few weeks of training, Mauktik saw a noticeable increase in their stamina and physical fitness. As soon as she saw this development, she added combat training to their programme. The boys first practiced hand-to-hand combat, and when they got better at it, they moved on to training with wooden sticks.

They had adjusted to their new lifestyle completely by the end of the third week, and they were approaching their training with unwavering dedication. Even Arjun, who at first had merely wanted to stay with his friends, gave as much effort to each task as his friends did.

In the fourth week of their training, Brahmarishi also observed their development and praised their exceptional achievement. "All three of you have been performing exceptionally well in your training," he said. "However, it's important to control your aggression and practice mental tranquillity to foresee your opponent's moves as you fight. You must master the skill of meditation in order to accomplish this. Your meditation instruction, which is crucial for opening the chakras, will start today."

The guys were thrilled to hear this because they realised that their tireless efforts were paying off and that they were getting closer to their ultimate aim.

The boys approached Brahmarishi to begin their meditation journey in order to activate their chakras after their morning yoga and asana sessions. They received thorough instructions on the procedure from Brahmarishi, who also told them to start with the lowest chakra and described the sensations they would feel when it was active. He underlined that they should move through the chakras step by step, ascending to the last one above their heads. They would be able to regulate their physiological functions and communicate with the universe if they could master this technique.

Their training proceeded, and as the months passed, the boys displayed extraordinary skill in every aspect of their curriculum. Mauktik was surprised by their fast learning and adaptation, which she had never seen in a human before. This confirmed her idea that they did indeed contain Janatig souls. The boys displayed exceptional agility, excelling with equal ability in combat, science, and problem-solving. While Mauktik was pleased with their improvement, she couldn't help but wonder which of them her father was, as none of them had any particular behaviour or habits resembling his. She remained attentive and observant, though. Arjun's decision to not accompany them on their journey was yet another remarkable observation. Despite this, she was astounded by his relentless commitment to every assignment and the fact that he never once complained. She could see that there was a really close link between the three buddies.

After residing in Jnañā-sthan for 8 months, all three boys had successfully attained the 5th chakra, known as the Visuddha chakra. Brahmarishi and Mauktik both observed a gradual transformation in their temperaments, characterised by a growing sense of tranquillity and empathy towards all things. In addition to their rigorous training, Mauktik and the boys found time to relax together, sharing stories and experiences. The more Mauktik got to know them, the more convinced she became that they were indeed worthy of the hopes and expectations that the Janatigs had placed on them. Over time, the four of them developed a strong bond of friendship.

As their adventure continued, Akash and Aditya frequently asked Arjun if he still wanted to go home when they were done. The answer from Arjun remained steady. On one occasion, Aditya asked a question that had been bothering him: "If you are inevitably going home, why go to such lengths in your pursuit of knowledge here? You may just go home and concentrate on your aspiring career. Why invest your time and energy in this pursuit when your long-time dream has been to become an astrophysicist?"

Arjun responded thoughtfully, stating, "Well, I really don't know. There are times when I think about following you on your adventure and supporting your efforts, yet a mysterious force keeps pulling me back home. But I also feel a deep, almost brotherly, connection to you both. Perhaps, if the ideas and theories about our shared former incarnations are correct, I am compelled to appreciate every moment we have together. My heart, however, is telling me that I must finally go back home."

The guys were trained in different crucial skills and improved their combat proficiency for several more months. Their progress this time, though, was distinguished by a little deviation. While Arjun struggled with it throughout these 2 months, Akash and Aditya gracefully unlocked the Third Eye chakra. Typically, their journey involved achieving a chakra within a matter of days' difference, and there were instances where Arjun outpaced his companions. However, this time, weeks went by with Arjun still trapped by the Third Eye chakra.

Akash and Aditya made rapid progress over the next 2 months, achieving not only the Crown Chakra but also the higher-dimensional abilities that allowed them to move forward with the Soul Star and Spirit chakras. Arjun was still battling with his sixth chakra in the meantime. He finally unlocked the Third Eye chakra 2 weeks later, though, proving the value of his unwavering commitment.

They had been in Jnañā-sthan for more than a year at this point. Only a few hours were set aside for the practice of other talents during this period; the rest of their time was spent in meditation.

On a calm day, Mauktik and her friends, the guys, discovered themselves enjoying a leisurely break under the swaying branches of the magnificent banyan tree. Their conversation centred on their personal journeys, monitoring their growth, and considering how far they had come. They gave Arjun words of encouragement, asking him to keep his unwavering focus during their reflective chat. It was clear at this point that the boys' viewpoint and behaviour had undergone a significant change. They showed a remarkable capacity for empathy, inner peace, and a great deal of patience while maintaining strict emotional control.

They were still talking when a sudden event caught their attention. A distinctive pendant on Mauktik's necklace that resembled a large water droplet suddenly released a bright aqua radiance and an unsettling, strange sound.

"I've been on earth for about 3 years now, and it has never reacted like this," she said, expressing her worry.

Akash inquired, "What is this?" with curiosity.

"This is a device through which my people can contact me via a particular radio frequency in times of emergency,"

Mauktik retorted. "It's difficult to tell how old this message is, but I hope everything is fine on my planet."

Mauktik pressed her thumb and index finger softly on the pendant's base, pulling the luminance of the pendant into the tips of her fingers. She carefully ran her glowing fingers over the back of her right ear, and immediately, her countenance changed dramatically, her skin turning paler.

"It appears that the Janatigs have stumbled upon a potential threat reminiscent of our previous encounters and expect another impending attack," she said as she relayed the alarming news. "They want me back immediately."

Aditya was worried and said, "What should we do now? Should we come with you?"

"No, you are not yet ready," Mauktik retorted. "Before we can contemplate taking you on board, you must first awaken your souls." Mauktik stood up, determined, saying, "I must seek advice from Brahmarishi," and moving towards their meditation sanctuary, with the boys following after.

Fortunately, Brahmarishi was approaching them already. The information Mauktik had received from her planet was passed onto him as well, and she asked for his opinion on the current circumstances. "Do not worry; everything will be fine," Brahmarishi assured them with his signature sense of calm and serenity. "Please, come with me."

Brahmarishi headed south, and with the rest of the gang trailing after, their focus concentrated on the distant waterfall ahead. They continued steadfastly for half hour, passing through a gorgeous meadow for a fair distance before moving onto a wide area of grassland. Throughout the expedition, a reverent stillness prevailed, and the party faithfully followed Brahmarishi's lead.

They saw the source of the river that meandered through Brahmarishi's meditation site as they reached the end of the grassy area. As soon as Brahmarishi crossed the stream, he started a calm procession through the chilly but bearable water that was coming from the high mountain glaciers above. As they got closer to the beautiful waterfall's face, their destination became more visible.

Brahmarishi came to a stop in front of the escalating downpour and took a thoughtful position. He closed his eyes, clasped his hands together, and began to softly intone mysterious words while standing in reverie. The waterfall's violent flow eventually ceased in response to his presence, and the water split in half. The divide eventually became wide enough for them to pass through. Brahmarishi resumed his movements, indicating to others that they should do the same.

After going through the waterfall, they went deep inside a cave, and as they did, darkness engulfed them like a thick cloak. Mauktik duplicated her previous actions by lighting up her clinched fist, ever mindful of her friends' limitations in the absence of night vision. They were able to easily move through the maze-like corridors of the cave thanks to this radiant light.

They had to move quickly because the cave was filled with sharp slopes, descents, and crevices. A gleam of light beckoned from the far end of the cave after persisting for another half hour. This glowing spot, clearly indicating the exit to the cave, was where Brahmarishi guided the way. The gang continued with unshakeable resolve, narrowing the distance to their target.

However, just as they were about to exit, Brahmarishi abruptly came to a halt. He took a brief minute to scan his surroundings before turning to the right. Mauktik and the guys were bewildered by this unexpected departure from the obvious exit, but none dared to ask questions, instead choosing to obediently follow their beloved guide.

Resuming their journey into the tunnel, they navigated the darkness once more, guided by Mauktik's blazing fist. The corridor became narrower with each step, adding an aspect of mystery to their already enigmatic journey.

After about 10 minutes of walking, the path became so constrained that they had no choice but to move sideways in a single file. They eventually reached a larger space, but it seemed to be at a dead end. All eyes were on Brahmarishi, who served as both their leader and compass on this mysterious expedition. Brahmarishi closed his eyes, joined his hands together, and uttered a quiet incantation without hesitation.

Two torches that were set up on either side of the chamber suddenly flared in response to his mystical prayer, illuminating the space with a warm, flickering glow. The stone wall in front of them started to shift and protrude in an amazing pattern that reached all the way to the cave's roof as they carefully listened to faint sounds coming from the rocky walls. After the turbulent transition was complete, the jutting rocks created a steep staircase that led to the upper reaches of the cave.

Brahmarishi said, "Please follow me and use caution as you ascend," with a serene air of authority. Observing Brahmarishi's effortless ascent, the boys eagerly followed suit, their prior training in navigating steep surfaces proving to be an asset. Brahmarishi skilfully removed a stone lid from the cave's roof, allowing himself and the others to escape after ascending about 30 stairs.

They emerged from the tunnel one by one, entering what seemed to be a completely different world. They discovered themselves in the midst of ancient ruins that were decorated with massive, towering pillars made of pristine marble that exuded an air of mystery and timeless history.

Brahmarishi led the group through the intriguing ruins after emerging from the cave, eventually taking them to a spectacular gateway-like structure. The majestic marble pillars that made up this architectural marvel's design gracefully formed an arch above it as it stood in a wide open space.

As he turned to face Mauktik, Brahmarishi said, "I sense the necessity of your departure for Ganagrah. You can easily travel back to your native place through this Gateway to Beyond. I am aware of your need for our young warriors' support, but you are also aware of their limited readiness. However, after they have successfully finished their training here, I will see to it that they arrive on Ganagrah in a timely manner. Please make the required arrangements in the meantime."

The grateful Mauktik said, "Thank you very much, Brahmarishi. Your advice and encouragement have made a lasting impression on me. I am glad that our meeting has demonstrated that my trip to earth in quest of Jnañā-sthan has proven fruitful."

Turning her attention to the young boys, she continued, "I cannot express the depth of my gratitude for having crossed paths with all of you. A crucial aspect of my journey has been getting to know each of you. I regretfully have to leave in the middle, but I am optimistic that we will meet again in our home, on Ganagrah." She took a gentle pause and continued, "I understand the decision you took, Arjun, but I still harbour hope that you'll follow your brothers' example and follow the same route. I bid you all farewell with these words and look forward to our upcoming reunion."

Mauktik elegantly moved, approaching the finely carved stone gate under Brahmarishi's direction. She again bowed low and touched her forehead to the Brahmarishi's feet as he extended his hands in blessing. She made a bow and joined her hands after turning to face the boys, and they returned the favour.

Standing beneath the arch of the gate, Mauktik awaited Brahmarishi's mystical invocation. As Brahmarishi closed his eyes and chanted softly, a beam of light channelled from his forehead, striking a small circular area meticulously etched into the gateway's arch. The gate appeared to change almost instantly, looking as though it were covered in a sparkling membrane of water that was floating over its surface.

Brahmarishi reassured Mauktik, stating, "You are ready for your journey." Mauktik bid the guys a heartfelt farewell, her eyes sparkling with gratitude and a radiant smile on her face. The guys waved goodbye with the same warmth. The water inside the membrane slowly started to emit a glow, which it continued to do until it reached a magnificent crescendo. Everything dissipated as the light faded gradually; the water membrane disintegrated along with Mauktik, leaving only the plain stone gate in its place.

After Mauktik left, there was a noticeable sense of loss among the boys. They followed Brahmarishi back along the same route, pondering the deep encounter they had just witnessed.

When they got back to their home, Brahmarishi left, leaving the boys to congregate on the veranda of their modest hut with their eyes glued to the setting sun. They had made great strides in controlling their emotions, but they were still fundamentally human, and a deep grief engulfed them at that precise time. But they never lost sight of the fact that they still had a long way to go.

The guys incessantly kept up their practice of meditation even after Mauktik left. On his spiritual path, Arjun, however, struggled with the Crown Chakra. He had the impression that, while in deep meditation, his attention had wandered to some vague extraterrestrial phenomenon. Though the time and location were vague, he had brief, hazy visions of a hospital while meditating. Arjun's mental state at the time did not trouble him, but it made him want to learn the solutions to problems he could not properly articulate.

Akash and Aditya tried to bring it up with Arjun, but he kept his inner thoughts to himself, delivering vague responses that hinted at a subtle uneasiness with his progress. Both Akash and Aditya noticed a developing sense of detachment in Arjun over time—a subtle shift that bothered them.

Four days after Mauktik's departure, Brahmarishi asked Akash and Aditya to meet him an hour before sunset, implying that more revelations on their spiritual path were on the way.

During the golden hour, Akash and Aditya obeyed Brahmarishi's summons, choosing not to alert Arjun because Brahmarishi had not given them any explicit instructions regarding him. When they arrived at their usual meeting place beside the river, the same tranquil spot where Brahmarishi frequently meditated, they found him seated, revelling in the ethereal light of the golden hour.

Brahmarishi addressed them as they approached, acknowledging their curiosity with a contemplative glance.

"You must be wondering why I have called upon you," he said. "Cosmic events are unfolding that require our immediate attention, and time is of the essence. Please come with me."

Brahmarishi began a deliberate journey toward the eastern horizon, where the rough terrain started. Akash and Aditya matched their guide's pace as they ascended the rocky terrain in his wake, doing it with commendable ease. They ascended the rough terrain for an exhausting hour until they reached the summit, which was also the highest point. The youngsters were in awe of the beauty that met them. They could see their tiny ashram below and the entire world spread out before them from this vantage point. In the distance to the south, the snow-capped mountains stood majestically, and they could see the glacier, the source of the river that cascaded into a waterfall.

With the sun throwing a relaxing orange glow and softly brushing the horizon, showering the entire Jnañā-sthan in a warm, yellowish-orange colour, Akash and Aditya took a minute to regain their breath. Aditya was unable to hold back his curiosity any longer in the face of this stunning scenery. He asked, "Brahmarishi, why have you brought us here?"

In a sombre reply, Brahmarishi said, "This location serves as the entrance to the Space of No Time. It is an empty space in the cosmos where the flow of time ceases to exist. There are no sources of light or discernible substances there. In that realm, time does not control how you live, and your body is not affected by life or death. Only your soul and thoughts endure. Make intelligent use of this area to realise your inner potential and awaken your spirit. Time stops when you enter this dimension. You can meditate at your own pace to awaken your final chakras. As soon as the last ray of sunshine strikes this revered mountain, the entrance to this realm will become visible. It only stays open for 3 seconds, and that only happens once every 3 months. You must therefore enter as a group as soon as you spot it."

When Akash and Aditya were informed of the presence of this unusual location, they both nodded in unison. As the sun fell below the horizon, a subtle enthusiasm appeared on their faces.

Akash and Aditya prepared for the crucial moment they had been anticipating as the sun elegantly dipped under the horizon, enveloping the steep terrain in an ever-increasing cloak of darkness. Brahmarishi, standing at a safe distance, observed with a knowledgeable attitude. There was a tangible sense of expectation.

Their persistent watch eventually paid off. A strange, shadowy oval window appeared in the air before them as the sun's final, waning beam stroked the summit of the hill. Despite having an oval shape overall, the shadow's borders showed some irregularity, as if it were simultaneously taking energy from its surroundings and radiating it.

As soon as the mysterious shadow appeared, Akash and Aditya wasted no time in leaping into it and disappearing into a pit of intense darkness. They found an odd separation from their physical bodies inside. They couldn't even call out to one another, as though their vocal cords were muffled. They were confused by the sensations in this area because they contradicted all their real-world expectations.

They started meditating in an effort to stay concentrated on their goal. They calmly recited their mantras in the privacy of their own minds, envisioning themselves in their normal contemplative postures. They could meditate in peace and quiet because there were no outside disturbances at this location. They were able to go into the depths of concentration because of the complete calmness.

As they immersed themselves further in meditation, they experienced a sensation of weightlessness, as if their physical bodies had dissolved into nothingness. Aditya, in particular, started to notice the subtle energy flow that was passing through him, searching for a source of inner vitality by weaving through the neurological pathways of his physique like tiny beams of light. As he continued his meditation, a soft, soothing warmth accompanied this profound connection to his inner self and enveloped him.

The transforming process evolved within him over time, progressively illuminating all 7 chakras in a sequential ascension, beginning at the basic base and ascending to the apex. Once ignited, each chakra radiated its own potency within him. This progressive escalation of the process unleashed an incredible surge of energy, comparable to the fiery fusing of atomic nuclei, and he radiated a brilliant white radiance comparable to that of a celestial star.

He felt as if his head had built an ethereal bond to the universe itself—a mysterious connection to the cosmos. He visualised a vast panorama of stars, galaxies, and constellations in this transcendental moment and then felt the fullness of these celestial objects as they assimilated into his very existence. He became a vehicle for this incredible presence as the procedure continued, and he felt a profound merger of his mind with another soul. He started to recall memories from a previous existence while in this enhanced state and vividly remembered the powers he had once wielded. The understanding that he had undergone a significant transformation—he had effectively awakened Atulya—was accompanied by a profound change in his perception. He also realised that he had attained the Soul Star and Spirit chakras, which was a significant turning point in his spiritual development.

A faraway, brilliant light drew Aditya's attention as his eyelids fluttered open in the vast empty space. He moved through the void with a grace that gave the impression that he had floated through it. As he drew closer, he saw Akash hovering in this limitless space, his eyes closed in intense meditation and reflecting his own brilliant splendour. It was clear that Akash had acquired the last two chakras as well. Akash's eyes focused on Aditya's form in front of him as they slowly opened up. Their eyes met as though they were sparkling gems, each illuminating the significant change they had each undergone. Aditya could see Akash mouthing words, but he was unable to hear the sound, which he construed as Ashvath's call to Atulya. As they drew closer to one another and held hands, the dazzling light that was coming from their bodies started to fade.

They gradually lost brightness until the entire area was reduced to an all-pervasive emptiness that was completely dark.

Chapter 13:

Home Calling

The sun had elegantly dropped beyond the horizon at the top of the cliff, spreading its fading hues throughout the scene. Brahmarishi took up position on a cliff's edge and kept a sharp eye on the activities taking place. In a surreal moment, he observed Akash and Aditya entering the enigmatic black shadow that emerged in the air, only to come out of it the very next second. Brahmarishi's smile was subtle but sincere; the two brothers' glowing aura was proof that they had succeeded in completing their task. The shadow dissipated into the atmosphere just as swiftly as it had appeared.

The two brothers approached Brahmarishi with confidence and composure, humbly bending to touch his feet and seeking his blessings. They then gave each other a sincere hug, with barely a trace of emotion showing on their faces because they had gained a condition beyond common emotions. But there was a faint undercurrent of joy in their expressions.

The star-studded canvas above them revealed its amazing beauty as the surroundings progressively turned dark. They had never before seen such grandeur in the sky, which was crystal clear. The area eventually fell into total darkness, and a celestial galaxy shimmered gloriously exclusively overhead.

"I assume you both are now prepared to travel to Ganagrah, where Mauktik awaits," Brahmarishi said to them.

"Brahmarishi, if you don't mind, we would like to spend the night here in Jnañā-sthan and set off for Ganagrah tomorrow," Akash replied in answer to their request. "Since we don't know when we will see our brother Achyut again, we want to be with him."

Warmly responding, Brahmarishi said, "Of course, as you desire, my child. Let's go down and eat dinner together."

The darkness had no effect on them as they headed down the hill along the well-known trail because of their improved perception, which made it an insignificant barrier. They arrived back at their starting point in about 20 minutes. Turning to Brahmarishi, Aditya made the suggestion, "Brahmarishi, we shall go and fetch our brother Achyut, and then we can have dinner together."

With a nod, Brahmarishi answered, "Certainly."

The walk from Brahmarishi's meditation spot to their hut was only a short one. As the night progressed, the surroundings faded into darkness, with only a few flickering diyas gracing the front doors of the huts. When Akash and Aditya arrived at their own house, they noticed Arjun absorbed in meditation on the veranda. Arjun's face was illuminated by the soothing glow from the diyas.

Arjun greeted them with a joyful smile as he welcomed his friends, his curiosity subdued by the sense of pride emanating from their radiant auras. As he got to his feet, Akash and Aditya approached and embraced him. Aditya expressed their desire to bid him farewell and spend one final evening together, while also expressing their understanding of his decision to decline their invitation to come along. "May you flourish and find success in your chosen path," Akash concluded with a message of goodwill. "We believe that one day, our paths will cross again."

Arjun admitted, "I will miss both of you dearly," overcome by grief. "I have no idea what I would do without you two." They kept holding each other throughout the subsequent silence, finding comfort in their connection. When Akash finally pulled away, he said, "Let's go to supper. Brahmarishi anticipates our arrival." With this agreement in place, the three brothers headed for their supper while savouring their remaining time together.

After dinner, they did what they always did: they went for a peaceful walk along the beautiful lakeside. While the area was bathed in a light glow, the moon's silvery brilliance danced across the surface of the lake, producing a dazzling spectacle that projected a soft glow on their faces.

Words were unnecessary in this nocturnal ambience, and they were wrapped in a profound silence, their emotions echoing with the peace around them. Each was aware of the others' silent thoughts, but they all shared the implicit knowledge that it was not the right time to express these feelings.

After a time spent in quiet contemplation, they returned to their hut. As the evening advanced, the soft glow that had emanated from their window gradually dimmed as they extinguished the lantern within, retiring for the night.

The following morning, as was his custom, Arjun awoke to the soothing symphony of songbirds before the sun rose. But this time, he awoke to find that his brothers were not there. He didn't appear to be upset when they left, but he felt a subtle pang of longing in his heart. Arjun continued his routine as usual, unsure of what to do now that they were gone. He started his day with a bath and then did his asanas and yoga poses. But he chose to visit Brahmarishi first before starting his meditation.

Arjun travelled to Brahmarishi's meditation spot as the sun rose and a new day began. There, he discovered the sage deep in meditation. Brahmarishi softly opened his eyes and smiled as Arjun approached, greeting him. With his palms clasped in respect, Arjun extended his own greeting. "Suprabhaatam, Brahmarishi," he said in greeting.

Brahmarishi returned the greeting and invited him to sit on the fresh, dew-drenched grass in front of him. "I had anticipated your arrival," Brahmarishi said. "Have a seat, please."

Arjun consented and sat down on the verdant soil. "It appears you may be unsure of your purpose here," Brahmarishi added. "I had hoped that you would finish your curriculum before deciding on your next step. However, the decision you make will always be yours to make."

Arjun paused for a second before posing his question. "May I ask you a question, Brahmarishi, if that's good with you?"

Brahmarishi encouraged him, "Certainly, ask whatever has been on your mind," with a grateful nod.

Arjun said, "Why does it appear that whenever I pursue something, I always have to go through more difficult challenges than others? There have been times when, in spite of my uttermost commitment, tolerance, and steadfast effort, I have fallen short of my objectives while others around me have easily accomplished theirs. We set off on our respective adventures together, but they succeeded while I failed. I've stayed here for a while just to be with them, yet even now I'm struggling. I have felt a profound sense of emptiness since they left. I don't want to stay here any longer, and I want to go home. Perhaps spending time with my parents will help ease some of the emotional strain."

In answer, Brahmarishi expressed compassion and acknowledged Arjun's feelings. "I am aware of the emotions you are experiencing. The solution to your initial query is included within the question itself. Your desire to spend time with your friends first motivated your intention to learn the discipline of meditation. However, your companions had a clear reason for mastering this skill—a reason potent enough to move them closer to their objectives more quickly. On a second point, it's important to keep in mind that we are constantly given an option, and that decision will determine the direction of our destiny. These decisions reveal our inner selves as well as the road that leads to our destiny. A determined person keeps trying until they succeed, seeing each failure as a step forward. Such a person carves a covert path to success after a run of failures. Faith is yet another essential component to bring with you on the journey. The key to success is self-confidence. If your only motivation for believing in something is to succeed, that thing will always elude you. Only when you stand firmly and, most importantly, truly believe in yourself can you attain true success. Only when a person has a sincere belief in a miracle or a prayer will they see results. The essence of what I have to say, my dearest Arjun, is that. You will undoubtedly find your way soon; I'm sure of it."

Arjun responded by expressing his gratitude. "I sincerely appreciate your advice, Brahmarishi. But a part of me wants to go back to my house. I choose to continue my journey in the land of the living." In order to obtain Brahmarishi's blessings, he bowed and touched his feet. "I've reached a major turning point in my life, and I will always value the things I learned here." Arjun bid Brahmarishi farewell, making the gesture with clasped hands while feeling conflicted inside, and then went back to his hut to collect his belongings. Brahmarishi silently observed Arjun's exit while maintaining a calm smile.

During his journey back to his hut, Arjun's thoughts were consumed by the wisdom imparted by Brahmarishi. He arrived at his hut without realising it when he got there while lost in thought. Arjun went inside the hut and started gathering his things and putting them in his bag. He took a moment to tidy up the living space, placing Akash's and Aditya's possessions in their respective bags and situating them in a corner.

After leaving his hut, Arjun went to Nishka's house with the intention of saying goodbye and thanking her for the information and help she had given them while they were there. After they parted ways, he set out to return to the mortal realm, using his memory as a trustworthy map to lead him back to the route they had taken to get to Jnañā-sthan in the first place. Arjun reflected on the profound lessons Brahmarishi had conveyed as he travelled along this well-worn path. He couldn't help but think back on the failures he had experienced throughout the course of his life, which were vividly replaying in his memory.

He finally reached the exit after walking for around 40 minutes. He considered the significance of his choice while standing in front of the exit. Arjun was well aware that leaving this area would make it nearly impossible for him to come back. As he considered the consequences of his decision, his quandary grew more complicated. He relaxed on one of the nearby trailside boulders after setting his backpack down. Within him, a fierce internal battle raged. Thoughts of someone calling him home began to take precedence over the urge to finish his meditation here, which tugged at his thoughts.

Arjun, firm in his choice, pulled his legs up into the padmasan position and began to meditate there, beside the trail, sitting on the boulder. He entered a state of intense reflection while reciting his mantras and gave in to the inner calling that had led him to make his decision.

The failures Arjun had experienced throughout his life came to mind as he sank into a state of intense concentration, carefully examining each one. He imagined a plethora of potential solutions he could have explored to overcome these hurdles. He continued with his meditation by influencing his attention to Brahmarishi's teachings and cultivating an unflinching faith in himself.

Three days had passed since Arjun commenced his meditation near the exit, during which he abstained from food and water. He pursued his inner potential and the limits of his own consciousness with sheer tenacity. He eventually had a similar breakthrough as Akash and Aditya did after gradually beginning to feel the same sensations they had while obtaining the Crown Chakra.

When he finally opened his eyes, he saw that the area was dimly lit. Arjun descended from the boulder where he had been meditating, unsure if it was the start of a new day or the end of the previous one. As he gazed towards the exit, his mind drifted away from leaving Jnañā-sthan. Even though he continued to feel as though someone was calling him home,

Arjun realised that with the Crown Chakra at his disposal, he could get home much faster even without leaving Jnañā-sthan.

Resolute in his decision, Arjun gathered his backpack and went back down the trail, turning around to get to the river stream to quench his thirst. The progressively illuminating sky gave away the sun's impending rise. When he arrived at the river, he cleansed his face by submerging his head in the cool water. He was reenergised after quenching his thirst, and at that point, he knew exactly what he should do next.

Arjun looked around for a quiet place and finally found refuge under a tree by the river. He took one more look at the grandeur of the natural world around him before closing his eyes. His body leaned against the tree trunk, looking to be asleep as he slipped into a meditative state. His consciousness, however, transcended his physical form, becoming a free being that floated in the air—an accomplishment known as astral projection.

Arjun found it to be a remarkable experience to float around freely in this otherworldly setting as he revelled in the sense of weightlessness and let go of his burdens to the physical world. He didn't waver, though, in his resolve to complete this specific expedition. He became fascinated by this astral occurrence because it allowed him to travel great distances in a very short amount of time, which inspired him to make the decision to return to his home.

Everything in the astral world appeared somewhat warped to Arjun as he rapidly flew through it, lacking the clarity he was used to. However, he was led inevitably in the right direction by an intrinsic sense of direction. He travelled through this astral realm, arriving at his parent's house after travelling along a path where the surroundings remained blurry.

After such a long time of staying away, Arjun was relieved and nostalgic to see his home again. Arjun, who was raised in a middle-class family, had always had a simple but satisfied existence as a result of his parents' careful attention to his requirements. His house had a simple design, a typical two-story construction with a total of six rooms. His parents resided on the first floor while renting out the ground floor. He entered their living room after climbing up the stairs.

Arjun entered the living room to find himself all alone, the room empty and stark. He noticed a framed portrait of himself on the wall adorned with a garland, which immediately caught his attention. The fact that his parents had already come to terms with his likely passing was a shocking reality. Despite the clear signals, he clung to the hope that his parents would still be waiting for him.

He was still gazing at his own picture and lost in thought when he heard a woman's voice coming from the room next to him. Unmistakably, his mother's voice could be heard. He dashed inside the room, calling out, "Maa." His mother appeared unaware of him, as she was preoccupied with a phone call. He realised he was in the astral realm, where he was inaudible to others in the physical world and remained unseen. But when he saw his loving mother, whom he had terribly missed while he was away, a deep sensation of delight poured over him.

Arjun looked throughout the other rooms of the home in search of his father since he was determined to find him, but his search turned up nothing. He assumed that his father was still away from the house at work. Arjun went back to the room where his mother was conversing and sat down next to her, enjoying the warmth of her presence.

Arjun listened intently to his mother's conversation over the phone. She responded, "Yes, Guruji," with a hint of worry in her voice. "I'm sorry for the previous disconnect; it appears there might have been a network issue. As I mentioned before, it has been well over a year since we lost Arjun, yet here we are, caught up in a maze of legal procedures. According to our attorneys, we are unable to file a claim for his financial assets until his mortal remains are found. We made every attempt to find him, deploying a large number of men to explore the entire hilly area, but in vain. This difficult process has taken a tremendous toll on our finances, and we are now dealing with rising frustration. We are deeply concerned about the outcome of our laborious efforts throughout the year."

A heavy sigh escaped her lips as she continued, "My husband and I are left wondering whether there is still a glimmer of hope for us to legally obtain the fortune that legitimately belongs to Arjun, as passed on by his actual parents."

Following this request, she fell silent, waiting for the person on the other end of the line to respond.

Listening to the entire conversation left Arjun in profound shock, a sensation that coursed through his entire existence. The realisation that the woman he had believed to be his mother for his whole life had been a lie left him completely perplexed. Acknowledging that the people he had shared his formative years with were not his genuine parents fuelled his urge to learn more about his biological family. Arjun's mind was racing with inquiries regarding his biological parents' whereabouts and who they were, feeding an insatiable curiosity that needed to be sated right away. He desired to solve the mystery surrounding his ancestry. He was unable to speak with his mother directly because he was on the astral plane, which put him in an odd situation. Any attempt to announce his presence can be misinterpreted as a paranormal occurrence, which might make her feel frightened.

Arjun came up with a different strategy to find out who his real parents were in order to get around this difficulty. After his mother finished talking on the phone, he gently put her to sleep so that he could stealthily look around their apartment for any hints about his true ancestry. Arjun's heart raced with eagerness as he started to look around the room, but he wasn't sure where to start looking for answers.

Arjun realised that even though he had been living in this house for several years, the idea of looking through his parents' belongings had never occurred to him. He began a methodical search, thinking that any hints as to his genuine parentage might be covertly tucked away in a safe place. He started by looking through the cabinets' drawers, where his parents usually kept critical papers, but he found nothing useful. As a result, his attention was drawn to the most possible repository: the cupboard. He could easily skip the necessity of a physical key to unlock it thanks to his astral form. His initial search remained fruitless as he sorted through the contents, including files and folders buried in a corner. Frustration and disappointment came as he worried that his quest for information about his biological parents would go unanswered forever.

However, when restoring the files, his keen eyes noticed a seemingly small blue file with his name scrawled in tiny letters in one corner—an item he had nearly overlooked. This discovery motivated him to look into it further. When he opened the file, he discovered a collection of paperwork referring to properties, and to his surprise, he discovered his own name there. Further examination of these records revealed important information about his birth parents' inheritance and possessions.

The discovery of his significant fortune and assets left him feeling overwhelmed, but his thirst for understanding about his true parentage remained insatiable. His eyes were drawn to a little secret locker hiding beneath a mound of clothing within the cupboard as he began to explore. Its small size stopped him from obtaining physical access or seeing inside. However, his unique astral form enabled him to bypass this barrier, allowing him to unlock it from the back.

When he opened the locker, he discovered a treasure trove of gold jewellery, some of which he recognised as belonging to his mother. Among these priceless gems was a jewellery box, which he had never seen before. At the simple touch of the box, an unexplainable sensation welled up within him, driving him to open it. He carefully opened the jewellery box while seated among the garments in the cabinet, showing two magnificent golden bangles nestled inside. Under the bangles was a folded white sheet of paper, which he carefully withdrew while keeping the bangles within the box. He unfolded the contents of the paper, his curiosity growing. The paper had a brief note addressed to his mother, Natasha. The message read: "*Dear Natasha, I must write to you under these circumstances, and I need your most urgent support. My husband passed away a week ago, tragically on the same day as our terrifying accident. Unfortunately, my own situation is severe, and doctors see little hope for my recovery. I have my six-month-old son with me, who is in good health. Unfortunately, I will not be able to care for him. I implore you to take in my son and raise him as your own. You are the only person I trust with this duty. My lawyers will contact you as soon as possible. I've written a will stating that when he reaches the age of 23, you will inherit half of our fortune. Please provide my son with all the love we couldn't. I'm afraid I won't make it until your arrival, which is why I'm writing you this note. With gratitude, Swara.*"

Arjun experienced a tremendous shock after learning the truth. He grappled with uncertainty, not knowing what to do next or where to turn. He returned to his physical form within Jnañā-sthan, overwhelmed by his newfound sorrow. He opened his eyes, attempting to calm himself and come to terms with the suffering he had just discovered. The sun had reached its apex, but the sky had become clouded, with a nice, chilly breeze gracefully moving his long hair.

His eyes remained locked on the river that was flowing in front of him as he considered the unrelenting march of time. In the 18 years since his birth, time has nearly erased all signs of his biological parents, leaving him with just bits of information. However, Arjun now has the power of the 7 chakras, enabling him to travel through time while residing in the fifth dimension. Months of continuous meditation and his developing knowledge of the cosmos had led him to this point, where he was thrilled with his newfound confidence.

He shut his eyes once more and dove deep into his own mind to begin a journey across the unknown reaches of existence. In his mind's eye, he envisioned the cosmos extending out before him as if he were looking for something in the vastness. His focus gradually grew sharper, leading his mental journey through clusters of galaxies and stars until he reached a location shrouded in complete darkness.

Arjun remained highly aware of his surroundings as he floated in the ethereal emptiness, despite the fact that everything was shrouded in impenetrable darkness. He gradually felt an overwhelming pull, drawing him further into this limitless void. The force pressing on him grew stronger and stronger, giving him the sense of falling into an enigmatic abyss. He felt as if he were falling through the darkness, hurtling towards an unknown destination.

In an instant, he was back within the familiar boundaries of the visible cosmos, speeding towards earth. As he entered the earth's atmosphere, he appeared outside a hospital near the emergency department. A tremendous bustle of activity developed in front of him as two accident victims were quickly hurried into the medical facility's emergency room.

Amidst the chaos, Arjun overheard a conversation between two people who were clearly medical employees dressed in clean white uniforms. They talked about a terrifying car accident that happened near the highway. Tragically, the man who had been driving the car had succumbed to his injuries at the accident site, while the woman accompanying him, likely his wife, clung to life but was grievously wounded. Her serious condition demanded that she be transferred to the Intensive Care Unit right away.

They noticed an uninjured six-month-old baby boy who had been properly secured in the back seat of the car during the accident, which added a ray of optimism to the otherwise bleak situation.

A couple of police officers arrived and stationed themselves outside the Intensive Care Unit, eagerly awaiting the arrival of the doctor. A doctor appeared from the ICU around 2 hours later, leading one of the officers to ask, "Doctor, we are here to investigate the accident. What's the condition of the woman inside?"

"It is difficult to ascertain her condition at this moment," the doctor said, his face filled with anxiety. "She has lost a lot of blood and has gone into a coma. Her injuries are significant, particularly in the cranial region. Despite the fact that we did surgery on her, her prognosis remains uncertain until she regains consciousness."

"Understood," The policeman nodded in agreement as he expressed confusion over the victims' identities. "Surprisingly, we have no information on the identities of the victims. At the scene of the collision, there were no cell phones, purses, wallets, or other objects that could have served as identification. They also appeared to be in a brand-new car that glaringly lacked a licence plate. Please keep us informed if the woman awakens from her coma while we continue our search for information and contact potential relatives."

The doctor nodded solemnly in response to their request and said, "Certainly."

In contrast to astral projection, Arjun's experience involved him only perceiving the complete sequence of events in his head rather than physically being present at the hospital. As he continued to meditate, his mental images revealed that a few weeks had passed within the hospital, and the woman had eventually awoken from her coma. Unfortunately, a substantial portion of her body was still paralysed. She quickly asked about her son's and her husband's health as she regained consciousness. The medical staff, however, hesitated when confronted with her inquiry regarding her husband's fate. A doctor finally mustered up the guts to break the devastating news of her husband's demise after repeated pleas. She was completely crushed by this realisation. The caring medical staff made a sincere effort to comfort her despite her immense sadness and brought her son to her side in an effort to lessen her suffering. She was overcome with emotion as she saw her son in good health.

As her health gradually improved and stabilised, the medical staff sought to gather information about her in order to contact her relatives or next of kin. She disclosed, "My name is Swara, and my husband and I are both orphans. We have no living relatives, only a handful of close friends. My husband's dearest friend has been residing overseas for the past couple of years, and the only person close to us is a friend of mine. You can find her contact number on my phone."

To this, the doctor responded with a note of curiosity, remarking, "It's quite peculiar, but the police reported that none of your personal belongings were discovered at the accident site. No phones, no purses, and no identification cards —even your car lacked a number plate."

Swara acknowledged the strangeness of the situation, stating, "Yes, we had just purchased the car, but it is indeed odd that all of our belongings have gone missing." Despite some difficulty, Swara managed to recollect her friend's phone number from memory and provide it to the doctors. They attempted to contact her friend but were met with disappointment as the phone was switched off.

The police also visited Swara during this time, asking about her home, her family, and the events leading up to the disaster. "I am really unsure about how everything took a tragic turn in an instant," Swara said as she recalled the incident. "We had recently traded in our old car for a new one and were driving back from an event outside the city. My husband was driving at a modest speed through the forests that night when it was pouring heavily. While looking back at my child from the front seat, something abruptly hit our windscreen. The entire windscreen went dark as the wiper blades worked to clear it. As a result of the loss of visibility, the car veered off the road. Everything went dark after that. I was hospitalised when I awoke."

"Do you recall seeing anyone in the area nearby prior to the collision?" the police continued their questioning. "We couldn't find any of your belongings, and we're concerned they might have been stolen."

Swara answered, "No, I don't remember anything like that."

"Okay, please take rest, and in the meantime, we will also try to find your friend," the police said in their conclusion.

The following day, Swara's condition suddenly deteriorated. She quickly lost consciousness as her blood pressure dramatically dropped. After a thorough study, the doctors came to the conclusion that there were accident-related delayed complications that led to an infection that damaged her organs. It was doubtful that she would live for very long because of her poor prognosis. Later that day, she was able to regain consciousness thanks to medication, but even then, she could tell something wasn't right.

Swara, determined to get her affairs in order, insisted on having the hospital personnel compose a note for her friend Natasha on her behalf. While composing the note, she urged the nurse to emphasise the importance of showering her son with all the love she couldn't provide. Thanks to one of her caretakers, Swara was also able to get in touch with a lawyer who helped her create a will specifying that her son would receive everything of her and her husband's assets, including their house, money, jewellery, and investments. But until he was 23, he wouldn't be able to access these resources. The appointed guardian would pay all of his expenditures up to that point. The guardian would get half of her son's inheritance when he turned 23. Tragically, Swara passed away that night.

The police successfully located Swara's friend, Natasha, who had been abroad for a week. Upon their return, Natasha and her husband were contacted by the police and received the devastating news of Swara and her husband's untimely demise. Natasha was utterly shocked by the tragic turn of events and felt a profound sorrow as she visited her friend for the last rites during her funeral. She was also apprised of the existence of Swara and her husband's son, Arjun, and the conditions of adoption outlined in Swara's note.

Natasha was unable to control her tears as she read Swara's touching note. Although Natasha and her husband had never considered having children, they didn't even hesitate to honour their friend's request. Without a second thought, they welcomed Arjun into their home. They carefully completed all the required legal steps to formally adopt Arjun and raised him as if he were their own child. They also made the conscious decision to withhold information about his biological parents until he was old enough to comprehend his history.

Arjun stepped back into the present moment and gently opened his eyes. Darkness covered the area as the sun had already set beyond the horizon. His heart was deeply burdened by the information regarding his parents. He never had the chance to meet them, but he felt a great sense of sorrow and longing for the parents he never got to be with. He never felt resentful towards his foster parents because he knew how well they had raised him and never once made him feel like he was not their child.

As Arjun set out on his journey back to the ashram, the night sky above him was adorned with a fabric of brilliant stars. The area was serenely calm, and a nice breeze murmured its welcome, refreshing him upon his return. His return seemed to be warmly welcomed by nature itself as the trail took him to the serene lake and the cool breeze swept over him.

He arrived at the ashram's familiar grounds after a leisurely stroll. While returning to her hut, Nishka spotted Arjun as he greeted her with a pranam. When she caught sight of his homecoming, her face glowed with joy.

After speaking with Nishka, Arjun moved in the direction of Brahmarishi's hut. He observed the sage leaving his home as he approached closer. Arjun and Nishka's conversation had probably been overheard by Brahmarishi. In order to get the sage's blessings, Arjun humbly knelt before him, placing his forehead softly on Brahmarishi's feet. The sage expressed his joy at Arjun's homecoming and gave a warm and welcoming response in return.

In response to Brahmarishi's statement, "I knew you would be back." Arjun said, "Yes, it seems I have some unfinished business here."

In agreement, Brahmarishi answered, "Yes, you do."

Arjun chimed in, "Brahmarishi, I have attained the Crown Chakra," anxious to share his development.

Returning the compliment, Brahmarishi said, "I am delighted you have reached this milestone. I hope you now have the self-assurance you need to work on the remaining chakras."

Arjun, with unwavering determination, affirmed, "Yes, but I shall rely on your continued guidance to do so."

In his characteristically loving attitude, Brahmarishi reassured Arjun, saying, "Of course, my child, I am here for you whenever you need it. You must be hungry, I presume. Have a full dinner first, and then we can discuss the rest tomorrow."

Arjun's face lit up with delight as he said, "Yes, that sounds wonderful."

They both left and headed back to their individual huts after that. After enjoying his meal, Arjun took a little stroll around his hut in the moonlight. His heart ached for his buddies this evening, and his longing for their camaraderie and the nightly routine they formerly shared only grew stronger. After some time, he went back to his hut and made himself comfortable enough to sleep for the night.

As the deep indigo canvas began to soften, painting the sky with a lighter bluish shade and a hue of reddish-orange at the horizon, Arjun woke up to the sweet melodies of the birds chirping in a melodious harmony. Maintaining his usual routine, he went to the river stream and took a bath. After completing his morning yoga and asanas, he went to meet Brahmarishi.

As Arjun made his approach to Brahmarishi's meditation place, the sky was pleasantly gloomy. When he arrived, he saw Brahmarishi engrossed in meditation. Instead of disturbing him with words or commotion, Arjun chose to position himself calmly in front of the sage, exhibiting incredible patience as he waited for Brahmarishi's meditation to be complete. Nearly 2 hours passed during this attentive watch, which came to an end when Brahmarishi opened his eyes.

Arjun didn't say anything because he was waiting for Brahmarishi's advice.

"I hope the wait wasn't too boring, my child," Brahmarishi said, breaking the stillness in a cool manner.

He was reassured by Arjun, "Not at all."

Brahmarishi asked, "Tell me, my child, what is it you wish to discuss?" in a peaceful tone.

"Today, I sense a profound change within me, one that has emerged during my time here," said Arjun. "On one hand, I feel obliged to reunite with my companions and aid them in their mission, but on the other, I feel a mysterious yearning pulling me in the direction of an unknowable destination. I seek your wisdom and counsel as I navigate these conflicting paths."

"Certainly, as I've previously stated, your choices carry significant weight, and they will ultimately shape your path," Brahmarishi responded. "However, in order to help you make a more educated decision, I suggest you thoroughly explore all aspects of your decision-making process."

"That corresponds with my own thoughts," Arjun agreed. "Would you be able to direct me to the place where my buddies acquired the final two chakras, if I may ask?"

Brahmarishi explained, "Well, the situation is a bit complex. The entrance to that place only becomes accessible once every 3 months, and we must await the next opportunity. Moreover, it requires clear weather conditions for the entrance to be visible. So, the odds of reaching that location are somewhat slim. I would prefer you to focus on achieving the Soul Star and Spirit chakras right here without my assistance. Always remember that worthwhile achievements often require patience."

Arjun acknowledged, "Thank you for your guidance. I will continue my learning journey here."

With a warm smile, Brahmarishi inquired, "Is there anything else I can assist you with?"

Arjun responded, "Actually, a thought occurred to me while I was sitting here, although I may not have paid much attention to it before."

Brahmarishi questioned inquisitively, "And what might that thought be?"

"Well, Mauktik said that Jnañā-sthan existed within the central prism area when she earlier detailed the universe cluster and the relative placements of our planet, Ganagrah, and Jnañā-sthan. If that's the case, then why does this place look so much like earth? There is a definite time difference between earth and this location, I've noticed."

Brahmarishi elaborated, adding, "Remember that Mauktik indicated that this space resides within the sixth dimension. Therefore, if you were to picture this place in 3 dimensions, it would be trillions of light years away from earth. However, earth and this realm merge within the sixth dimension, establishing a connecting point on earth that connects the two realms."

"So, through the Himalay?" asked Arjun.

In agreement, Brahmarishi said, "Yes, exactly. Additionally, this location rotates clockwise in parallel with earth; therefore, the apparent time discrepancy is not caused by a gap in time. It is just the case that when the Himalay on earth face the sun, it is night here, and vice versa; thus, it is not an issue of time difference."

Arjun continued with curiosity, "And what about the sun? I'm assuming that the suns on the two worlds are separate. I believe that light doesn't travel between other dimensions."

Brahmarishi clarified, "You're right that light doesn't pass between dimensions, especially in the visible spectrum. As a result, the sun that you see here is different from the sun that you view from earth. Although distinct from the sun, the star you see here is almost identical to it."

Arjun analysed this and inquired, "So, what is it called?"

With a quiet smile, Brahmarishi said, "Suryadev."

Arjun chuckled as he realised the play on words. He respectfully bowed, touched Brahmarishi's feet, and then made his way back to his hut.

Arjun arrived at his hut, demonstrating a strong sense of determination and mental preparedness for his meditation. He carefully closed the doors and windows and covered any openings, sealing off all possible sources of light. The outcome was that the room went completely dark. He took up a meditation position in the middle of his hut, closed his eyes, and started reciting mantras. Gradually, he cleared his mind of all thoughts, allowing himself to sink into emptiness and immerse his consciousness in the boundless void.

His body gradually started to feel lighter as a result of this process, and energy started to radiate from each of his 7 chakras. He imagined a multitude of tiny, coloured light rays moving inside of him. More of these luminous threads started to emerge over time, weaving intricate patterns inside of him. He started to realise that these light rays contained information, much like memories, when he focused on them. One exceptionally dazzling white beam stood out among the many others for him. Focusing more intently on that, he watched as this dazzling ray got brighter and more intense until he could make out a picture within it. He found himself being drawn deeper into the brilliance with increased focus until it abruptly broke forth in a blinding flash, covering everything in whiteness. He became aware that he was in a whole new universe as his vision adjusted to his surroundings.

When Arjun woke up inside his consciousness, he found that he had transformed into the appearance of a young boy with significant physical similarities to Mauktik, replete with luxurious, Arjun-like long hair. He was lost in the peace of his surroundings as he wandered aimlessly through a little patch of forest, his lips creating a melodic and deeply calming tune that resounded throughout the quiet forest.

As he continued his carefree exploration, his senses were captivated by the presence of a magnificent, azure-hued flying insect, resembling a dragonfly but distinguished by wings that shimmered with all the brilliant colours of the rainbow. Enchanted by this abstract creature, he set off on an unplanned mission to capture it, relentlessly pursuing the speedy and nimble bug as it dodged and hovered in the air. The bug's quick movements forced him to push himself harder in pursuit.

Arjun had no idea that his courageous pursuit had taken him deep into the forest, where there was a higher density of greenery. As he continued in his search for the elusive insect, something unexpected happened: he abruptly disappeared from view amidst the enormous underbrush, which would have been a confusing sight for anyone watching. Unknown to them, the young Janatig had accidentally fallen into a hidden pit concealed within the vegetation, succumbing to unconsciousness in the process.

After some time, he began to slowly regain consciousness, his groans ringing through the darkness as he became increasingly aware of the pain in his body. To his surprise, he discovered himself nestled inside the same hole he had unintentionally fallen into. A sliver of light crept through the aperture above, but the majority of it was still blocked by the vegetation. The upper edge of the cavity, from which he had plummeted, seemed to be about 45 metres away from the ground, where he lay now. His surroundings were completely hidden by the darkness that surrounded him. The pain flowing through his body gradually subsided as his eyes adjusted to the darkness, and he was able to make out the interior of the cavern. He summoned his determination and attempted to stand up. What was in front of him resembled a vast underground room; he had never read of a place of this size in any of his historical writings or codexes.

The ceiling in his prior position was too low to allow a decent vision, so he shifted a few steps to the side to better his perspective of the space. With each step, he noticed the presence of water at his feet; its current was slowly flowing in an evident direction. He made the decision to explore his underground surroundings after fully realising that help would not likely arrive from his fellow Janatigs, who rarely travelled through this remote forest. He likewise understood that returning to the inaccessible opening above was impossible.

Desperate to find a way out of this enigmatic underground zone, he set out on a two-hour excursion into the perplexing darkness, following the path of the running water.

As he progressed deeper into the tunnel, the landscape began to descend while the water level slowly climbed. He eventually arrived at what appeared to be a dead end, with the water now approaching the level of his waist. He considered alternative escape routes while reflecting on his dilemma. He stuck his finger into the water to taste it while searching for hints. He noticed the water's undeniable salinity, which pointed to the sea as its likely source. This revelation strengthened his notion that there must be a road carrying him out to the open sea.

With this renewed hope, he submerged himself beneath the surface of the water, peering into the depths. There, in the liquid darkness, he could make out a few flimsy rays of light shimmering. He swam determinedly towards these illusive glares, his strokes fuelled by expectation as he swam deeper into the vast expanse. His desperate search for an escape required him to sink even deeper into the murky depths.

When he got to the light's source, he discovered himself in a room enclosed by the underwater cave, where more illumination awaited him. He eventually emerged onto the open sea, met by the distant glimmer of Ridham's light, after navigating the maze-like twists and turns of the cave's underwater pathways. As he proceeded to swim towards the surface, his head broke free from the water's grip, revealing a vast expanse of open sea.

However, Arjun was lost because he could not see any land or his own island; all he could see was a portion of the cave sticking out of the sea. Puzzled by the extent of his underground journey, he swam toward a rocky outcrop of the cave and climbed its uneven surface, eventually taking a seat atop one of its jagged stones. Surprisingly unaffected by the obstacle of returning home, he felt a peaceful confidence that a way back would offer itself in due course. Exhaustion weighed heavily on him as he dried himself off, forcing him to seek relief. Climbing farther within the rocky structure, he located an enclosed space where he could rest undisturbed.

The symphony of waves breaking against the craggy cliffs, combined with the endless expanse of sea stretching to the horizon, filled Arjun with a profound sense of happiness. He leaned back in the cool shade and closed his eyes to appreciate the tranquillity. He eventually gave in to fatigue and fell into a light slumber after being soothed by the peaceful surroundings for a while.

However, his pleasant snooze was unexpectedly interrupted by a noise other than the steady lullaby of the waves. He was abruptly roused to consciousness, jumped to his feet, and quickly searched the surroundings for the origin of the strange sound. Despite keeping a close eye on everything, he saw nothing unusual. He tentatively sat back down, but the enigmatic noise interrupted him again, suggesting that something or someone else might be there.

Once more rising to his feet, he crawled covertly in the direction of the mysterious sound's source, able to now identify its location on the other side of the cave. Moving cautiously around the corner, he ultimately arrived at another confined room similar to the one he had occupied previously on the other side of the rocky elevation. As he continued his cautious approach to the source of the sound, he noticed a dark, serpentine tail gradually tapering to a pointed tip. As he drew nearer to get a better look at the creature, he unintentionally disturbed some gravel, sending a cascade of stones tumbling down the slope and making a cacophonous disturbance. In response, the creature went into high alert and retreated behind one of the cave's boulders. In an effort to make his good intentions known to the mysterious creature that was inside, Arjun maintained a steady posture.

After a brief pause, the creature carefully peeked out from behind the boulder but quickly withdrew into hiding. In that brief time, all he could see were a pair of brilliant, round, and flaming eyes accompanied by a set of horns. Despite a minor surge of terror, he carefully regulated his nerves and approached slowly, taking a seat in front of the hidden creature. He maintained a calm posture as he started to whistle his favourite tune, which had been a part of his life since he was young. The melody began with calm and soothing notes, instilling a sense of lightness and peace in the ambience. It moved with grace and fluidity at a deliberate and slow pace. He had used this specific music to communicate with animals for years, and it had not failed him on this occasion as well. Gradually, the creature re-emerged from its hiding place, revealing its enigmatic form.

The creature had a serpentine body with overlapping scales that had a muddy yellowish-green hue. Its facial features included a pronounced nose and mouth, framed by prominent whiskers, and crowned by a pair of horn-like projections atop its head. A thick mane cascaded down its head and neck. The serpentine form had tiny arms and small, powerful feet, with a thorny tail completing its odd morphology.

His whistling paused as he wrestled with the surreal nature of the creature before him. His book knowledge claimed that dragons had become extinct millions of years ago, making this meeting even more incredible. The dragon, on the other hand, moved slowly forward, emerging fully in front of Arjun and coiling its tail over its legs. The melodic music had clearly transmitted a sense of confidence, convincing the dragon that Arjun had no ill intentions. Arjun resumed his whistling, and the dragon and Arjun maintained a steady and steadfast look, creating an odd bond in their extraordinary encounter.

Since he was a young child, he has used his innate ability to comfort and communicate with animals. This special talent aided the dragon in his quick development of trust. Their friendship grew stronger over time, transforming Janatig and the dragon into loyal friends. Arjun discovered not just friendship but also a new home inside the same cave, only venturing into the water for food. In order to ensure a supply of fresh water, he even developed his abilities in rainwater harvesting. Over time, he learned how to communicate with the dragon, and he gave her the name Jwala. As Arjun and Jwala set out on expeditions beneath the sea's surface, their days together were packed with aquatic excursions and underwater adventures. These expeditions frequently took them to the underground lairs of other dragons, with each visit veiled in secrecy, a condition Jwala imposed once she was confident of Arjun's discretion.

Through their secret encounters, he learned that Jwala struggled with her growth as a dragon and was frequently the target of taunts and exclusion from her dragon peers. She was only 1800 days old, lagging behind her peers who had already learned to breathe fire. In order to avoid raising any red flags among the other dragons that lived beneath the water, Jwala was very cautious whenever she came to visit the Janatig. He was incredibly happy to be with Jwala, since it satisfied a need he had been longing for since he was a young child. They developed a connection with one another that helped them when dealing with their communities, and they also learned how profoundly they could communicate their deepest ideas with one another. This newfound friendship acted as a spark, giving him the self-confidence and faith he had long desired but struggled to develop in his younger years. He carefully worked on the abilities he had found difficult in the classroom during his alone time, even devoting some of his leisure time to meditation.

His continuous support extended to Jwala as well, serving as a source of inspiration and direction for her efforts to develop her skills. Jwala eventually mastered the ability to breathe fire, steadily honing her skills with his guidance. The Janatig boy meticulously developed his own dormant abilities, bringing them gradually to the forefront. Their collaboration took the form of friendly combat challenges, with the goal of improving the efficiency and precision of their respective skills. His devotion to meditation remained unwavering, as he wanted to unlock higher-dimensional energies and forge a profound connection with the universe. Jwala's development continued to evolve as time passed, with each passing day leading to further growth. She also experienced a noticeable increase in size, indicating her continued development.

Thousands of days passed as time resumed its relentless march. In the midst of one of Arjun's meditation sessions, an unexpected realisation burst through the serene depths of his consciousness: a catastrophic threat loomed aggressively over his world. He went deeper into his meditative state in an effort to solve the mystery of this impending danger, since he was both intrigued and somewhat alarmed. His internal thoughts depicted a terrifying scene of imminent disaster, with torrents of rage set to envelop his planet. What scared him to his core, though, were the horrific visions of his siblings' lifeless forms. No Janatig had ever experienced an unnatural death, so this was a sharp departure from the past for his species. Despite having travelled far from his ancestral home, Achyut's love for his brothers remained strong. Given the sophistication of their race and the imposing stature of his siblings as some of the most powerful Janatigs on the planet, the idea of their demise seemed inconceivable.

Achyut made a determined effort to remain calm as he wrestled with these distressing thoughts. He started meditating again, hoping to gain a better understanding of the threat's proximity and impendingness. He was startled out of his deep meditation at that same moment by a cacophonous noise that broke the peace outside. He hurried outdoors to find out what was going on and was horrified to see the sky aflame from the constant bombardment. A startling realisation—the unsettling worry that the impending danger may somehow manage to get past their planet's powerful defences—took hold after a comprehensive assessment of the situation.

Achyut was determined to take action in order to protect his home planet from imminent danger. He was motivated by a growing sense of urgency and the uncomfortable possibility that this threat might be connected in some way to the deaths of his brothers.

In the face of impending danger, Achyut urgently beckoned Jwala, realising that her speed was essential for reaching their island swiftly. They needed to act quickly because there were around 15 kilometres between the cave and their island. He cried out to his trusted dragon companion, but she did not appear, much to his amazement.

Achyut used his psychic powers to create a mental link with Jwala in order to bridge the communication gap. Through this connection, he learned the unsettling truth: she and other juvenile dragons had been locked down by their adult counterparts in the ocean's depths. Due to their concern for their young ones, the adult dragons reacted to the alarming foreign threat by taking such action.

Achyut planned a clever escape strategy in this desperate position and used his psychic abilities to communicate it to Jwala. Concurrently, he went into profound concentration, seeking solutions to the impending threat and ensuring the safety of his brothers. The seriousness of the situation, however, became evident because he was in a hurry and couldn't afford to carefully sort through the data one piece at a time. In a decisive moment, Achyut harnessed his higher-dimensional powers, splitting his existence into multiple realities. His search for crucial information was sped up because of this extraordinary skill that allowed him to travel between many parallel worlds at the same time. He formed five separate entities, giving each one a particular purpose. One investigated the circumstances that led to his brothers' potential danger, while another investigated who was planning the attack and its motivations. While a third entity looked at options for completely avoiding the issue, a fourth one pursued tactics to save them. As Achyut set out on this multidimensional journey to face the impending threat and protect his family, the fifth entity prepared to look into worst-case scenario backup plans.

During the roughly hour-long duration of Achyut's meditative state, he effortlessly absorbed the knowledge acquired by each of his unique entities, positioning himself to face the impending threat with a thorough comprehension of the circumstances. At the same time, he learned encouraging news: Jwala had managed to escape the adult dragons' grasp and was on her way to meet him. True to her reputation, she appeared at the cave's entrance within the next 5 minutes. Achyut jumped atop Jwala's robust back, ready to continue on their quick voyage. Jwala's amazing prowess was on display once more as they soared above the water's surface. She navigated the stormy seas with incredible dexterity, even in the face of the tempestuous ocean churned by the continuous disturbances, a monument to the abilities she had cultivated over the past days. Their escape carried them towards the mainland, and despite the difficulties created by the dangerous waters, they persisted. The voyage took a little more than an hour, but with their combined dedication and Jwala's extraordinary powers, they got closer and closer to their destination.

As they got closer to the coast, they noticed something unusual: a swarm of robots dropped from the sky in fast succession. To avoid the mechanical assault, Jwala made a quick left turn, navigating for an area within the sea defined by a heavily forested clump of trees, their roots protruding above the water's surface. She expertly constructed a way towards the mainland, where she dropped Achyut, by navigating through this maze-like underwater arboreal expanse. Achyut signalled Jwala to remain hidden in the shade of the trees and resist joining the oncoming conflict on the battlefield. But as soon as he stepped foot on the land, a startling and unanticipated ambush appeared, with robots appearing as if by magic and unleashing a merciless assault. Achyut skilfully evaded their strikes and retaliated with resolute resolve, engaging in combat, while Jwala gave critical help by incinerating the robots with her fire breath. For a substantial amount of time, the fight consumed Achyut and Jwala's attention and energies, but Achyut quickly noticed a change in the robots' strategy. They moved backward immediately, all moving in the direction of the mainland. Recognising the importance of his mission, Achyut urged Jwala to remain hidden on the beach, away from bystanders, and he dashed towards the main land. As he ran towards the robots, he realised he was already late, causing him to change course in the direction of Prajñā.

Achyut quickly began a search after arriving at the specified site, but his familiarity with the storage structure allowed him to find the appropriate equipment with ease. He decided to use a laser injector along with some iron dust.

He grabbed hold of these things, accelerated his flight, and ran towards the burning battleground, where his brothers and the defensive team were heroically fighting the invading robots.

Achyut arrived on the battlefield from an obscure corner, where he noticed Ashvath had already exposed the robot's power source, causing his brothers to prepare for a coordinated assault. Achyut, who had loaded the iron dust into his laser injector during his quick approach, started a lightning-fast sprint as soon as he realised he was too far away from the approaching target. Gaining speed, he launched himself into a stunning leap in the direction of the important objective. Achyut's voice burst out in a frantic yell, pleading, "No....." As Ashvath and Atulya moved closer to the power source, he shot the iron-dust-infused laser injector into the air, sending a dazzling beam of energy in the direction of the exposed power source. Ashvath and Atulya gazed skyward in the middle of their aerial manoeuvre, drawn by the voice's familiarity, but their response was delayed. When the iron dust made contact with the power source's core, the fusion of heavier elements there had already started, beginning a slow self-implosion and releasing a massive amount of energy. Even before the weapons wielded by Ashvath and Atulya could touch the susceptible power source, a tremendous explosion erupted, preceded by a chaotic roar.

It took only a fraction of a second for the star-like power source to succumb to its own gravitational forces, at which point it momentarily carved a tiny cosmic tunnel into reality. The three brothers, who had been in close proximity to the power source, were killed by the explosion's devastating force, which also threw their lifeless bodies with great force. Simultaneously, the freshly formed cosmic tunnel had an insatiable appetite, sucking in all matter and energy in its immediate vicinity. This included the ethereal soul energy of the dead brothers, which it absorbed into its churning jaws before ejecting these soul energies down the other end of the tunnel, hurling them towards a remote and uncharted realm. This procedure was followed by a massive gamma-ray burst that resulted in a powerful explosion of radiant radiation.

Jwala kept herself submerged beneath the water's surface as instructed by Achyut, effectively protecting herself from the terrible effects of the shockwave and the accompanying radiation. However, as the deafening roar echoed through the air, she was prompted by curiosity to look above the surface of the water, where she saw the enormous cloud formation that the terrible blow had produced. Her sharp eyes also noticed something being ejected from the explosion and hurtling out towards the ocean. She quickly made her way to the area of impact, propelled by an instinctual sense of worry. However, what greeted her was a heartbreaking scene that destroyed her very core. Jwala's eyes welled up with tears as she saw Achyut's lifeless body floating on the water's surface. She produced a mournful and resounding wail, her anguish resonating through the atmosphere as she was overcome by the emotional impact of the moment. Jwala delicately carried Achyut's lifeless body in her small claws beneath the sea's embrace, enveloping him in the depths as she struggled with the crushing loss.

Arjun slowly opened his dazzling blue eyes, illuminating the entire darkened space where he had been deeply absorbed in meditation with stunning azure luminescence. His memory of Achyut's entire life gave him a great sense of completion and, at last, gave him a strong sense of purpose. He realised the intense longing for his true home that had been calling to him all along in that pivotal moment, a realisation that had eluded him up until this point.

Arjun got to his feet and unlocked the door to his simple hut after realising that a significant amount of time had passed during his meditation. His eyes were forced to close in response to the fresh illumination because he had been imprisoned in the darkness for a long time. The tremendous brightness from the outer world poured in. It became clear that a dramatic transition had taken place as he looked over the altered terrain. The view extended as far as his eyes could see—a perfect scene covered in a pure layer of sparkling white snow and illuminated by the radiant rays of the sun. Arjun saw a significant change in his own appearance as well. His face was framed by a lush beard that had grown, and his hair had grown out into a waterfall of long, curly strands. He took pleasure in the tranquillity that encompassed him as he sat on the veranda and observed the serene beauty of nature. This inner quiet chimed in perfect harmony with the newly discovered clarity of his objective.

Arjun was sitting in peaceful concentration when he noticed Nishka slowly making her way towards her own hut. He addressed her and greeted her with a heartfelt and reverent gesture by joining his hands. The sight of him after such a long absence filled her with emotion, and she couldn't help but express her feelings, adding, "It's a delight to see you again, especially after such a long absence. It's been almost 3 months since you last left your hut, and you've undergone quite a makeover."

Arjun said, "Ah, I had lost track of time," in a voice that had a calm and profound resonance. "It's so lovely to see you once more. I had also hoped to pay a visit to Brahmarishi."

"Certainly, he is currently in his place of meditation," Nishka said with a pleasant demeanour. "You are certainly welcome to pay him a visit."

After giving it some thought, Arjun said, "I believe I should take a bath before that."

Nishka gave a contented nod before advising, "Of course, as you wish. However, keep in mind that the water might be really cold."

Arjun said, "Thank you," and joined his hands in namaskaram before walking towards the river with Nishka's advice as his guide.

Arjun returned to his modest hut after immersing himself in the cold embrace of the river's chilling waters. He dressed himself in fresh, ashram-appropriate garb and set off on his mission to see Brahmarishi. Even though he continued on the same path that led to his respected guru, his once-familiar surroundings had been completely altered by the immaculate area of shimmering white ice.

As he approached Brahmarishi's meditation sanctuary, he noticed the lack of snow in that area, which stood in stark contrast to the surrounding winter beauty. Brahmarishi sat in deep thought within this quiet niche, absorbing the sight of the snow-draped terrain. The sage's countenance was blessed with an effulgent smile, indicating his awareness of Arjun's approach.

Arjun walked up to his beloved guru and bowed respectfully before reaching out to touch Brahmarishi's feet in order to get the blessings that had led him on his transformative path.

"Brahmarishi, I hope everything is fine here," Arjun warmly said as he initiated the talk.

"Indeed, and it appears that you are doing well as well," Brahmarishi said. "Your expression says a lot."

As he responded, "Thank you," Arjun's face softly smiled. "I have succeeded in harnessing the force of the Soul Star and Spirit chakras, Brahmarishi, and have awakened Achyut. I have finally realised my true worth and the breadth of my abilities."

"I am delighted to hear this news," Brahmarishi retorted, his expression beaming with pleasure. "You must be delighted to reunite with your friends on Ganagrah, as it appears that your reason for being here has been fulfilled."

After giving it some thought, Arjun spoke, "While that notion surely crosses my mind, I must say that I have imbibed significant wisdom from you, this hallowed area, and its residents. The extensive knowledge and experiences I have obtained are gifts I will always be grateful for."

"I am certain that you will excel in all your forthcoming endeavours," Brahmarishi said, nodding in understanding.

Arjun expressed his gratitude for his mentor's advice by saying, "Thank you."

Brahmarishi asked Arjun, "How soon do you plan to depart for Ganagrah?" in an effort to learn more about his travel schedule.

Arjun responded, "I am in no hurry, and I will stay here as long as my presence is required," to demonstrate his lack of haste.

"Excellent!" Brahmarishi said in his heartfelt reply: "Then why don't we have lunch together? You can start your journey to Ganagrah tomorrow."

Arjun nodded in agreement while grinning, and they both went on to have their meals together.

As one chapter of the story concludes on this side of the world, the stage is set for the start of another on the other. In this vast cosmos, countless things have happened. Mauktik has begun her voyage back to her home planet, while Akash and Aditya have joined her in assisting the Janatigs in their preparations for an impending and epic conflict. A new dimension of existence stands poised for revelation, awaiting its unveiling. In parallel with Achyut's reawakening, a significant change occurs within the realms of Ganagrah, another dormant spirit awakens from its sleep, its slumber having continued since the time of Achyut's untimely demise, down beneath the infinite depths of the ocean. The same round, blazing eyes are once again alight and glancing out at the world.

I am sincerely thankful for your time. Please share your thoughts to mystl391@gmail.com *when you have a moment - your feedback means the world to me.*